CHASE

D.L. Hays

ISBN-10: 978-0999109601
ISBN-13: 099910960X

Cover design by Les (Germancreative/Fiverr.com)
Interior design and typesetting by D.L. Hays
Edited by Nancy(EditorNancy/Fiverr.com) and Patricia Garner
Reviewed by Bryan Jansen and Dee Hays

To Mum, Bryan, and Eric.
I love you.

FEAR IS TORTUROUS.
IT ERODES OUR MINDS AND EVEN OUR BODIES UNTIL WE ARE
SO DAMAGED THAT WE FALSELY PERCEIVE THE WORLD AND
PLUMMET INTO A STATE OF BELIEVING WE ARE TOTALLY
HELPLESS.

CHAPTER ONE

LOCATION: USA
TIME: PRESENT DAY

Darkness filled the sky and covered the earth as Sarah Daniels slept inside her room. Though normally surrounded by the proud, boisterous melodies of the crickets and frogs serenading her from the pond outside her window, tonight Sarah lay surrounded by a firm stillness; silence. Nothing stirred about. At least, that's what one would think....

Amongst the quietness, a dark form moved. A spidery, dark foot slowly left the shadows. Like a tiger lurking in the woods with silent footsteps, a huge, dark man crept toward his victim. With swift, evil movements, his hands flew from his side and grabbed her neck.

Sarah saw him standing above her, the white of his evil-intending eyes glaring at her through the darkness, but she lay still as though frozen. She told her hands to move–to punch him–but they would not move. She told her voice to scream, but nothing came out. It was as if her entire body rebelled against her. She was paralyzed. She could only remain frozen in terror as the man's hands became tighter and tighter around her neck.

Suddenly, a dog's bark pierced through the darkness. The man vanished. Sarah sat up in bed; breathless and sweaty. *Was that real? Or had it just been a dream?*

LOCATION: RURAL SOUTH CAROLINA
TIME: TEN YEARS PRIOR:

A cool summer breeze tossed Sarah's brown hair around her bronze face hiding her brown eyes. She was not bothered by the obstruction of view, as she sat silently listening to a Bible teacher and focusing her eyes on the table in front of her.

She listened as the teacher shouted about remaining pure in a sinful world, his face red with anger as sweat beaded off his weathered face. Though he quoted Scripture, his words were angry and focused on people who did not believe the same as he did. He called other religions "sinful" and said that the followers would "die and go to hell."

I disagree and just want to be invisible, Sarah thought as she watched an ant crawl across the picnic table in front of her. But being invisible was not possible—the teenage boys sitting at the tables across from hers kept stealing glances in her direction. Though her gaze was down on the table and she never made eye contact, she could feel their eyes on her.

The Bible teacher paused and Sarah looked up briefly. She caught the eyes of one of the young men at the other table.

Wow, she thought, as she took in his light blonde hair, blue eyes, and beautifully tanned skin. She quickly looked back down at the table and continued watching the ant dart along the creases in the wood table. She could not stop thinking about the young man. *His eyes...there is just something about them that seem sweet, or maybe peaceful.* She stole one more glance and then stopped. *He cannot notice me looking at him. He may say something to me later.* She felt a knot grow in her stomach at the thought. *No—he cannot talk to me. He looks sweet, and I don't want something to happen to him.*

The teacher dismissed the class with a final prayer and led them to the ball field to play softball. Sarah felt a gnawing feeling in the pit of her stomach; she had been through this so many times before. Because she had not spent her early years in the United States and was now being homeschooled, she had no experience playing US team sports—no access to online databases that would have information on how to play them—and the people at the church had no patience or desire to teach her. Instead, they would force her out onto the field and enjoy making jokes when she messed up or did something that seemed illogical. It was humiliating and there seemed to be no way out of it since everyone was forced to play. She reasoned, however, that this could be averted if she was to hide from them or direct their attention elsewhere.

She slowly followed the other students down a hill to the field, lagging behind just far enough to break away from the group as they reached the field. She walked into the nearby woods, hid behind some bushes, and watched from between two branches. As usual, the other teenagers lined up for the teachers to decide who would be on each team. She knew the drill: the students would line up and the harsh-voiced Bible teacher would start at the front of the line and slowly walk to the end while yelling out the numbers one and two repeatedly and pointing to individual teenagers.

The teenagers who saw him point to them and say one were on the first team; the others were on the second team. It did not really matter though because the teenagers always pretended to forget their numbers and joined the teams of their cliques, never straying outside their social circles.

Though it had been hard, Sarah was beginning to accept the glaring truth: she would never be in one of those circles. Though she desired to connect with her peers and though she usually got along well with people, her situation made it impossible to connect with anyone.

She stayed behind the bushes until the game started. Luckily, no one noticed she was gone, and now it was too late for them to add a player. She considered going out into the open but, the woods were significantly cooler than the field since the tall oak trees blocked the summer sun. Sitting on the ground, she pulled her knees up toward her chest.

There was a rustle of leaves beside her. She looked up to see the blonde guy walking towards her, his blue shirt and khaki shorts blowing in the summer breeze. "Hey," he said with a slight Southern accent as he approached, "not playing?"

Sarah shook her head and shifted her gaze to his feet. "Not really my thing."

He pointed to the ground beside her. "Do you mind if I join you?"

She paused and quickly scanned her surroundings as

though looking for someone. "Y—you don't want to play the game?"

He shook his head. "Not really. I've never been one for sports."

Her thoughts whirled around inside her head as she suddenly found herself unsure of what to do or say. She wanted to talk to this guy. His sweet and polite demeanor contrasted greatly with the harsh-toned people she was accustomed to seeing in this area, and she wanted to know more about him. But something was stopping her: *What if Richard sees!? I can't have him spot me talking to this guy. It's too big of a risk.*

She paused a bit too long because the blonde guy shifted his weight, as though preparing to leave. "It's okay, I can go; I don't want to bother you." His voice was polite and humble.

"No, no," she said, suddenly regretting her hesitation, "you are fine. I would love for you to join me." She moved over slightly to provide a place for him next to her—more out of habit than necessity given there was a direct view to the field regardless of where he sat down on the ground.

He sat down beside her and stretched his legs out. For a few moments there was silence. "So," he paused, "if playing sports isn't your thing, what do you like to do?"

Sarah was speechless. *Is he really talking to me? Asking me what I like to do?*

"Piano," she finally managed to say, her voice a little

louder than she anticipated and her accent suddenly appearing. "I play the piano."

"Seriously?" He smiled excitedly. "That is awesome! How long have you been playing?"

"Hm, that's a hard one," she paused to think, "um, probably since I was about six."

"Wow, you must really love it then."

She smiled. "Yes, I do. What about you?"

"I'm into music too." He looked back out at the field and watched as one guy hit the ball and sent it soaring into the outfield. "I sing and play guitar."

"That's nice," Sarah said while her eyes began scanning the field in a pattern that made it seem as though she was searching for someone.

"Yeah," he responded, glancing over at her. "Are you okay?"

"Yeah," she responded and quickly continued the conversation so as to avoid similar questions. "How long have you been singing and playing the guitar?"

"I've been singing most of my life but I've only played the guitar for about two or three years. I'm not that great at guitar yet but schools like people to have an instrument of some kind, I guess."

"Schools—so you are going to college?"

"Yeah, I am one day."

"Where?"

"Not sure yet. My parents want me to try for a school in New York, but I don't know."

"Too far from home?"

"No, I've always loved traveling, but I'm just not a huge fan of big cities." Sarah's lips formed a silent "oh" as she nodded. He continued, "So what about you? Going to college?"

"Yeah, I'd like to."

"For piano?"

"No, I want to write one day, but I also like animals so I may go to college for biology to become a veterinarian."

"Gotcha, you could do both. You could be a vet and a writer. I bet vets have tons of awesome stories."

She looked skeptical. "You think so?"

He smiled again. "Oh yes, imagine the many stories they come home telling. From the owner who makes excuses about why his dog ate chocolate to the girl who is upset her dog is barking too much."

"Hm," Sarah responded, a sneaky smile dancing around her lips, "I am not sure those sound book-worthy exciting."

He laughed. "Hence why I'm not a writer; but I bet you'd be able to do it."

She smiled but then turned back to the field. This time, she spotted a shadow near the woods across the field. Her entire body tensed.

"Are you okay?" His tone of voice was gentle and she could feel his gaze on her face. "You look scared."

Wow, how could he pick up on that—no one else has ever noticed. Should I be honest? Or is he just another person who is going to hurt me? Is he real?

Without thinking, she shook her head. "No," she said quietly, "I—I'm—I" she stuttered, not quite able to find the words to say. *What can I say? That my adoptive father, Richard, is crazy and hurts me and I'm scared of what he'll do if he sees me with you?* Though it was the truth, she shuddered at the amount of trust she would have to give this guy she had just met and at the amount of pain she would have to endure if her father somehow found out she had told him.

"It's okay," he said gently, clearly seeing how much she was struggling to find words. "You don't have to tell me." He paused for a second. "Why don't we just change subjects—will that help?"

A small, sheepish smile stretched across Sarah's face; she nodded but her eyes still watched the shadow.

"Okay," he said, "what's your name?"

"Sarah," she responded, somewhat absently as she

watched the shadow move slightly.

"I'm Chase," he paused, clearly seeing she was watching something. "Is it something in the woods?"

She nodded. "Yes, and–and–and," she stuttered, "I've got to go. Don't follow me."

"You okay? Can I help you?"

"No!" she said, stronger than she intended.

He looked shocked for a moment before suddenly springing into action by digging in his pockets. "Wait," he said, "Just one second, one second," he pulled out a somewhat wrinkled napkin and a pen. He began scribbling something down. "Look, I don't know what's going on, but you're clearly scared and–even though I just met you, you seem like a nice girl. I don't want to see you scared. So, here's my number and info. If you need anything–a friend, someone to talk to, anything– just give me a call. Okay?"

She opened her mouth to say something, but no words came out. Instead she just nodded, slipped the napkin inside her pocket, and then scurried to the field. She walked to the fence and stood beside another girl who was there watching the game. Clearly, the girl must have come in late because she was part of the main clique and was often sought after to play with them. Because people in that group rarely spoke with her, Sarah knew that a long conversation with the girl was not likely but she hoped it was possible to maintain a conversation just long enough that her father would think she had been conversing with the girl and not with

Chase—the repercussions would be far worse if he discovered she had been talking with a male.

"Hello," Sarah said in a friendly but shy tone of voice with a slight accent. The girl looked over at her, let out a dramatic sigh, turned up her nose in disgust and walked away, throwing her long, blonde hair over her shoulder as she walked. Sarah swallowed hard. She had expected that reaction since it was not unusual for the girls at this church to act that way toward her, but she had hoped there would have been at least a little more time to make it look like they were having a conversation.

Richard approached, his beady green eyes looking up and down Sarah's body and giving her a look that she knew all too well. *He is testing me. He's going to say something innocuous and then gauge my reaction to make sure I have not made a friend well enough to connect with.*

"Meetin' folks?" His drippy Southern drawl disguised the undertone of a threat.

"Um," she responded, her tone of voice giving no emotion, "most people are busy with their friends." She felt his arm go around her back, his cold finger stab at her spine—it was his signal that he was ordering her to walk. To an outsider, it looked like it was a gesture of endearment—simply a father's hand on his daughter's back—but, if Sarah disobeyed and did not move fast enough, he would jab it harder and harder into her back muscles until it was too painful to resist. She walked forward. "It is time to go?"

"Yep," his voice was low, a signal that he knew she was hiding something. She cringed. *It's going to be a hard night.*

And it was indeed. Sarah had not even sat down in the backseat of the car before he started quizzing her about who she had spoken to.

"I saw you and that girl gettin' along. She seemed pretty nice," he said.

What? She was not—she turned her nose up at me and walked away. What part of that is nice? she thought but stayed quiet.

"Speak!" he screamed. She could tell his anger was rising—he hated to be ignored and the moment he thought she was ignoring him, his anger boiled.

"S—sorry," she stuttered. "She was fine."

His face expression calmed slightly. "Good. Now, who else did you talk to?"

"Not many—everyone was busy with their own friends." *Wrong answer, Sarah,* she thought to herself the moment the words slipped from her mouth. *I admitted that I talked to someone besides that one girl. He is going to want to know more.*

"Not many? Who? Speak, Sarah! Speak!" He screamed; her muscles tightened. *Whatever you say, do not tell him about Chase. He will hurt that poor guy. But does he know already? Did he see us together and is he just trying to get me to admit it? If that's the case, then if I do not mention it, the pain will be worse.*

"I told you. They were all busy in their own cliques with their friends."

"Right." His voice was sarcastic. "Busy with their friends—of course they were! But that doesn't mean you didn't talk to them." He slowed the car down to stop at the traffic light and turned right. Their house was only a short distance away on the left.

She stayed silent a little longer, unsure of how to respond. This, however, seemed to anger him more. "Sarah! Tell me what you told them. I know you told them! I saw you talking to that girl. What did you say? Speak!"

His anger was growing even stronger. She was alone with him in the car and feared what he would do next. "I walked up to her," Sarah's voice was calm for she knew that she could not show her fear, "and I said hello. She didn't say anything to me and just walked away."

"Psht!" he said, forcefully pushing the air through his teeth, "likely story." He drove the car close to their house but, to Sarah's surprise, he continued past it.

"Where are you going?" she asked.

"None your business," he snapped.

Fear built up in her gut and feelings of helplessness began to gnaw at her. *Where is he taking me and what is he going to do?* She sat still and watched as he drove the car a couple neighborhoods away and pulled into the back parking lot of a church. The parking lot was wooded and the summer sun was reaching the horizon, making the parking lot dreadfully shaded and increasingly dark.

He pulled the car next to the trees and stopped. With fury, he opened his door, slammed it, and walked over to Sarah's backseat car door. He opened the door and used his body to block her exit as he spoke from between clenched teeth. "You know me well enough, little girl, to know that I don't like being played with, lied to, or messed with. When I ask a question, I want a direct answer—not some B.S. answer. Now," he paused, "tell me what you told her. Speak!" His voice was so angry that she knew it was just a matter of seconds before he got violent.

He can't know I'm scared. He can't know I know he is going to try to hurt me. I can't let him know how this affects me or he'll only do it more.

"I told you the truth, sir. I told her nothing. The only thing I said to her was hello."

"Right! Sure you did!" he screamed. "That's just a bunch of bull." Suddenly, before she knew how to react, he pushed her body to the side. But the seatbelt caught and refused to move her beyond a certain point.

"D**n it!" He pushed the button to the seatbelt; it let go, but he was only angered more.

Before she knew what was happening, her body was flat against the backseat and she could not move. He was pinning her hands down with his giant body. She felt paralyzed.

"Tell me right now or everything you know will change. I provide for you—I give you food and shelter and all you do is mess with me. You never appreciate anything!"

Her heart was beating fast, her stomach rumbled in pain, and her whole body ached under his weight, but she could do nothing. She was utterly helpless in his grip.

"Excuse me—excuse me, sir?" A female voice pierced through the scene from outside the opened car door. He sat up and looked outside. Frozen with fear, Sarah stayed lying down. "Is everything okay, sir? We saw ya parked here and wanted to make sure ya weren't havin' car trouble."

"I was," he responded, "but I think it'll be okay now. My wife is on her way to come pick me up."

"Ya sure? We can see what we can do—I believe we've got jumper cables in our trunk."

"Naw." Richard brushed the air with his hands. "I'm a mechanic so I'll be able to fix it. I just need to get some of my tools from my shed."

"Okay," the lady's voice sounded hesitant, "but ya sure? How far away is your wife? We could drive ya if ya wanted."

"Naw, she ain't far away. She'll be here in no time. Thank ya though."

"Okay, well, if ya change your mind, the preacher usually comes to the church around this time on Saturday nights, so he'll be here soon and can help ya."

"Okay, thanks." With that, Sarah heard the other car drive away. *Okay, the preacher is going to be here soon—he will not want a witness.*

Richard stood up; he slammed the car door behind him, walked around to the driver's seat, and sat down. For several long minutes, he said nothing and neither did she. After what seemed like hours, he cranked the car and headed home.

<><

Though he did not try to get an answer again, he punished her in other ways. For over a month, he forced her to stay in her bedroom day in and day out— no contact with the outside world. He even refused to let her use the telephone or computer. The only time she was allowed out was to eat—and the food was scarce—and to go to church. Her mother, a soft-spoken woman, was far too weak to stand up against such a violent man and always crumbled beneath his beady eyes.

However, Sarah kept that crumbled napkin, and when Richard was away or asleep, she wrote letters to Chase. When her parents left the house for errands or to meet with someone, she snuck out of the house and trekked through the woods to another neighborhood and to an abandoned house. Though the mailbox was tattered and worn, the mailman still delivered mail to it and she dropped her letters into that mailbox. She always found a letter from Chase there as well. The words he wrote made her smile. He was such a nice person that, as the years stretched on, he made her wonder: *Does a better life than this exist? Can someone really love me?*

CHAPTER TWO

The sun commanded its bright rays to spiral down to the earth below. Though the rays landed in many places, no island felt them quite as strongly as that of Chaiti. The island nation faced the fact that its many crops were becoming smaller and smaller due to these fiery rays that were rarely met with opposition from clouds. Despite the drought, the villagers still seemed to bring up enough produce to stock their small but busy open market located in the middle of the dirt plaza not far from their clay huts.

Watching the crowd of people bustling about the market, one could become blissfully unaware of the stark, cruel war the Chaitian people had faced over a decade ago. That war had left their democratic government in shambles, overthrown by an insurgency that no one could have predicted would have had the means, skills, or knowledge to conquer such a target. But the insurgency—known as the Mashottiís—had triumphed that day. Since then, the island nation had not been the same. The native Chaitian people were repressed, unable to speak their native language or practice their customs, and they faced constant discrimination—so much so that many had devolved to denying their heritage. However, there was still a small war smoldering beneath the surface of these repressed people who were yearning to have their culture back. The impact of this smoldering was so contained that few villagers allowed it to influence their daily lives—at least for now.

Ajahadé made her way down the dirt road between the huts and toward the market. Wiping the sweat off her brow, she squinted in the sunlight as she approached the market bustling with people, mainly women and children with a few men scattered about carrying items and selling goods. She walked up to a table with island fruits. Keeping her eyes on the fruit she gradually nodded to the man behind the table without getting eye contact since the Mashottiís did not allow women to make eye contact with men without permission. Though her eyes looked at the fruit as she had greeted the man, it did not take long for them to dart from the fruit and onto her surroundings.

She observed the crowd. Many women and children were hurrying about gathering goods. Closer to her position, she saw a small boy walking quietly beside his mother as she selected fruit while another child stumbled and fell over his sister who was trying to sneak some food off the produce stand. Ajahade's gaze darted to the other people standing about. She scanned each face to determine if any of them looked familiar.

That is when she saw her friend Jarah some distance ahead. Jarah—a pale, thin woman—always looked ill and tired, perhaps because she was truly malnourished or because she was constantly trying to keep her four active boys and one infant son under control. Her husband was a farmer and was often off in the fields working hard to get his dry fields to produce at least something to sell. Most of her time was spent doing housework and raising the boys.

"Hi, Ajahadé!" Jarah said excitedly, in French, as they approached.

"Hi!" Ajahadé responded. "How are you?"

"We're doing well—"

Before Jarah could finish, one of the boys interrupted, "Look, Aj! We got a mango!"

"Oh wow, you did! It looks yummy. Are you going to eat it?"

"Yeah," the little boy responded, his curly hair bouncing as he nodded his head up and down, "Momma says we are going to cut it and eat it."

Ajahadé smiled. "That sounds like a good idea."

"Yeah," he replied, "or it could be a ball!" and with that he sent it flying through the air.

"Jkika, no!" Jarah responded, but it was too late. The boys threw the mango from one to another until the youngest boy missed. The mango dropped to the ground with a thud and burst.

Quickly, the boys rushed in and began eating the pieces of the mango, not even bothering to remove the dirt. "Oh, this is *so* good!" Jkika exclaimed. "Aj, you want some?"

"No thanks," Ajahadé responded with a smile and looked at her basket full of fruit. "I have plenty of my own to eat." She paused, "Actually, there is no way I can eat all of this—do you guys want to come back to my place and visit for a while? I can cut this up for us to eat."

"Sure!" Jarah responded, and they departed for Ajahade's hut.

LOCATION: UNITED STATES OF AMERICA
TIME: PRESENT DAY

The summer sun glared down on the earth below as Sarah drove her car around the familiar curve in the road. Her music was blaring out the opened windows while Zeus, her big black dog, remained stretched out across the entire back seat. He was completely unaffected by the sound of CJ's hit song "I'll Always Be Here" roaring around his ears.

The roads were nearly empty, populated with only two cars along the road that turned off to different stores. Nevertheless, Sarah constantly checked her rearview mirror. It only took a moment for her to spot a car approaching from behind her. Though still a good half mile away, the road had become just flat enough that there were no obstructions in her view. She checked ahead of her and carefully watched as the car behind her got close enough for her to read the out-of-state license plate. *Okay,* she thought, *not a number I've seen before.*

Nevertheless, in her typical fashion, she kept her eye on the car as she made a turn. It followed. She took another turn, but this time the car continued straight. Sarah continued watching for the car to reappear but it did not. After several long country miles, she let out a breath of relief. *Guess we're fine,* she thought as the familiar gate came into view.

Approaching the gate, she entered a code into the box and watched as the gates opened, clearing the way for her to enter the Mychael estate. Moving forward, she watched the mirror to ensure no car had slipped in

CHASE

behind. Then she followed the familiar asphalt driveway, lined with oak trees, to the end and stopped outside the large house. "Okay, Zeus, are you ready to see Dr. Mychael?" Zeus' ears perked up and he stood up ready to exit the vehicle.

"Dr. Mychael, are you home?" Sarah yelled as she entered the massive foyer with stone floors, Zeus trotting along behind her.

"I'm in here, dear," the retired psychologist said from the kitchen. Zeus darted around Sarah and ran toward the kitchen. "Oh hi, Zeus!" the older woman said, her soft voiced excited. "How are you, buddy?"

"He was so excited when he saw your house," Sarah said to Dr. Mychael as she walked into the large kitchen with its marble countertops and state-of-the-art stainless steel appliances. She walked towards the tall and thin older lady who was now bent over petting Zeus behind the ears.

Dr. Mychael's wrinkled face stretched to form a beautiful smile. "He's such a sweetheart." She glanced up at Sarah. "Oh honey," her soft voice grew heavy in concerns. She stood up and walked over to give Sarah a hug. "You look so tired."

Sarah hugged her back and instantly felt a rush of warmth and love similar to the feelings she got when her own biological mother had hugged her in the past.

"What's wrong?" Dr. Mychael's bright blue eyes looked at Sarah with great concern.

Sarah turned away and bit her bottom lip. She couldn't help but think of what had happened the night before when she had looked up to see the man with spidery limbs emerge from the shadows and reach for her neck. *Was that all a dream? Or was someone really in my house? What would have happened if Zeus had not barked?*

In her typical fashion, Dr. Mychael respectfully waited for Sarah to speak. "I—I'll tell you later."

"Okay," Dr. Mychael said quietly and slowly turned to look at the teapot that sat on the stove. "I was making tea and it's almost ready. How about I finish this and we can go sit on the back porch and talk about this?" Sarah nodded.

A few minutes later, the two women were outside on the back porch that overlooked Dr. Mychael's beautifully landscaped flower garden—complete with a small fountain—sipping tea and munching on small tea cookies. For several minutes, they sat in silence, absorbing the beauty of the garden and the gentle breeze provided by the overhead fans.

"So dear, what is going on?" The older woman's voice was kind and gentle as her thick gray hair swayed in the breeze.

"I—I had another flashback, I think," Sarah responded, her voice trailing off.

"How did it happen?"

"Well," Sarah paused as Zeus walked up and bumped

her knee before lying down on the stone patio beside her, "I was asleep and I felt this shadow over me. Then, there were hands coming toward my neck, but I couldn't move. I tried to scream but nothing came out." Sarah bit her bottom lip as she struggled to hold back the emotions. "I–I felt helpless."

Dr. Mychael's gentle eyes watched Sarah's face, showing her concern without her even uttering a word. Sarah continued, "I was paralyzed. Nothing–nothing would move." Sarah felt her whole body shiver. "Th–then Zeus barked and the man vanished."

"So it was a dream?"

"I think so," Sarah responded, "but I don't know. I got up and I searched my house. I didn't see anything out of the ordinary."

"And you had locked your door?"

Sarah nodded. "But my windows were open since it was such a nice night and my air conditioner wasn't working."

Dr. Mychael nodded. "And you searched your whole house thoroughly as well as the yard?" Sarah nodded. "Have you heard from him?" Sarah shook her head, knowing that Dr. Mychael was referring to Richard. For several long moments, Dr. Mychael thought. After what seemed like several minutes, she spoke, "Well, honey, I suspect it was a dream. Still, if you feel unsafe and want to stay here, you know that you're welcomed to do that. You know you'll be safe here."

"Thank you," Sarah said her voice soft. *Safe. What a foreign concept.* The words of Richard came streaming back along with the vision of his beady eyes as they spoke the words, *"If ya ever leave, know that ya will never be safe from me. I'll find ya."*

"Have you seen or heard from anyone related to him?"

Sarah shook her head. "No, but I can't seem to shake this feeling."

"What's it like?"

"It's like I'm helpless. I feel scared again."

Dr. Mychael looked thoughtful. "And why do you think that is?"

"I think it's because of that dream—it triggered something in me and now I'm on high alert again. I'm checking my mirrors compulsively and memorizing tag numbers and watching the faces of everyone I see and asking myself if I've seen them before or not."

The older woman nodded. "I think that is completely valid and normal, Sarah. After what you have been through, it makes sense that this would stimulate those feelings and actions. After all, those actions are what saved you in the past when he tried to find you."

Sarah nodded. Dr. Mychael was right: those actions had saved her two years ago when Richard had sent people to find her. Though they were strangers to her, they had appeared in the same places several times and she had noticed. That's when she had left, again—

fled, to another side of the country before finally coming back to the East Coast. Now she was in North Carolina working at a local retirement home. Dr. Mychael had been in rehabilitation at the retirement home for a broken hip last year and, though she was now back at home, Sarah continued to check on her regularly and help her with household chores, as needed.

"Don't ignore those feelings, Sarah," Dr. Mychael continued. "They didn't lead you wrong before; however, do not let fear control you either. It's a hard balance but you must not let fear rule your life because if you do, he's winning. And fear also makes us do strange things."

Sarah thought for several long minutes before responding, "You're right. I'll try not to."

At that moment, Zeus heard a noise in the distance and stood up to look. Realizing it was a squirrel, Sarah looked at him. "Go get it!" she said and watched as the huge dog darted towards the squirrel. The squirrel ran up the tree and Zeus stopped at the trunk of the tree. Both animals stared at each other. The standoff lasted for several minutes before Zeus gave up and walked back to the women.

Sarah stood up. "Well, I'm going to go get to work on the house."

"Okay," Dr. Mychael responded. "Thank you so much, honey. Let me know if there's anything I can do to help, too."

"No, no," Sarah responded. "You just sit there and

relax. I'll take care of the house chores."

Dr. Mychael smiled. But before Sarah could stand up, the phone rang. "I'll get it," Sarah said.

"Mychael residence, this is Sarah speaking," she said into the phone.

"Hi Sarah, it's John." It was the familiar voice of Dr. Mychael's grandson. "How are you?"

"Oh hi, John! I'm doing well. Your grandmother and I were just finishing drinking some tea on the porch."

"Nice! It isn't too hot there?"

"It is hot, but the fans give us a nice breeze."

"Ah, I see," he responded. "I forgot about those. They do help a lot."

"Yes, for sure. Anyway, do you want to speak to her?"

"Sure. Thanks, Sarah."

"No problem! Give me one moment and I'll get her for you," Sarah said and handed Dr. Mychael the phone. Sarah smiled as she watched Dr. Mychael's face light up as her sweet, calm voice said hello to John. The bond between John and Dr. Mychaels was very strong. Sarah could see the love radiate from Dr. Mychael every time she spoke to him over the phone or even talked about him.

<><

The sun was bright again several days later as Sarah approached the gate of the retirement village where she worked. Pulling her car inside the gate, she watched behind her to ensure that no car had slipped in. Then, she followed the long winding road between small homes to a large brick building where most of the residents lived.

Pulling into a parking spot, she stopped and looked back at Zeus. "All right, my man, are you ready for work?" The dog instantly perked up his ears and stood, ready to go.

A nice breeze darted along the parking lot as Sarah and Zeus approached the entrance to the brick building. Several white rocking chairs sat outside, making the space along the outside of the building seem like it was more of a porch than a sidewalk. Several residents sat outside, chatting among themselves. One of the older men, sitting in a rocking chair, looked up and saw Sarah approaching.

"Hey, Sarah!" he said, his voice cheerful and excited to see her. He lifted his hands in a broad wave as a huge smile stretched across his wrinkled face.

"Well hi, Mr. Two! It sure is a nice day, isn't it?" Sarah responded as Zeus trotted up to the man and sat down for a rub. Mr. Two petted him behind the ears.

"Aw, yes it shore is! Wish it t'was a tab bit cooler though." He looked down at Zeus. "How does he do it anyway? Don't'cha think he gets hot in all that fur?"

"Oh, yes, he definitely gets hot. The poor thing will have his tongue out in a minute, but that's why he's got me. I keep him cool, ya know? I take him inside."

"Aw, yea," Mr. Two nodded as he ran his hands down the dog's back. "You're right, you shore do spoil that lil' one, don't ya?" He smiled. "Back when we had dogs on the farm," his voice trailed off for a moment as he looked over the parking lot and towards the pond that stood on the other side, "back on the farm, them dogs nev'r went inside. They stayed outside all year long. When they'd get too hot, they just go jump in the cow pond. Come back stinkin' like hog heaven." He shook his head. "No way my wife was a lettin' them in her house." He wrinkled his nose in disgust.

Sarah laughed. "Oh yes, if Zeus ever did that, he'd be finding either a bathtub or a doghouse outside."

Mr. Two laughed and then switched subjects. "What'cha got on the agenda for today, Ms. Sarah?"

"Well, the ladies and I are doing manicures and then we have a band playing at 3:00. You should join us for the concert; it's in the activities room down the hall."

"You and those ladies," he smiled, rocking back in the chair again, "always doing somethin' to look purdy. You know, my lady looked awful pretty last time you took her to the beauty parlor. Couldn't keep my eyes off 'er."

Sarah smiled. *The spark is still there between those two.* "Well, she is a natural beauty and you're a lucky man."

A big smile stretched across his face again, exposing his few teeth. "Yes, ma'am, ya got that right."

"Well," Sarah said, still smiling, "we better get inside. Can't keep the women waiting, you know?"

Mr. Two smiled and gave Zeus a final pat. "All right, big guy, I'll see you later then."

<><

"Do you want some brownies, dear?" Dr. Mychael said from the kitchen several days later. "One of the ladies at church made them and they are very good."
Sarah shook her head. "Thank you but I had better resist. I have not been exercising as much lately."

Dr. Mychael cut a piece for herself. "Okay, well, would you like to join me in the library?"

"Sure," Sarah responded, picking up her teacup from the counter and following the older woman down the hall and into the large library. The room always fascinated Sarah. It had large, oak bookshelves lining the walls that held books from all over the world, along with artifacts Dr. Mychael had brought back from the many countries she had visited. Large Italian leather chairs sat along the side of the room near the large set of windows.

The two women had spent hours in this room going over each of the items and their stories. Dr. Mychael's descriptions were always so vivid that Sarah felt she had been taken to a completely different world. Glancing at the far bookshelf, Sarah saw the small hand-carved figurine of a warrior that Dr. Mychael had received from one of the African tribes she had helped. Beneath it was an elaborate vase received from another tribe who had been highly grateful of her aid. And then Sarah spotted a new item: a medium-sized, intricately detailed cuckoo clock hanging from the only part of the wall that did not have shelves.

"Is this new?" Sarah asked, pointing to the clock.

"Yes, actually, it is," Dr. Mychael responded. "John brought it back from Germany for me."

"Neat! Why was he over there?" Sarah asked, knowing Dr. Mychael probably would not tell her much. Despite the fact that Dr. Mychael and her grandson were very close and talked almost every day, Dr. Mychael would never answer questions about his career or why he was constantly traveling. Sarah was not sure if Dr. Mychael knew and wouldn't say or if she simply did not know herself. Either way, Sarah had learned not to push or ask too many questions.

"For work, I believe. He said it was nice over there. He's been before and always talks about how much he likes the pretzels and pastries."

Sarah smiled. *Such a guy…he goes to a country rich in historical sites, amazing architecture, and art and he is most fascinated by the food.*

"I told him that he should pop his head into one of those cathedrals or castles though. The architecture over there is so lovely. Well, at least it is to me."

"I agree," Sarah said. "I've heard that it is really beautiful over there."

"Yes, indeed." Dr. Mychael sat down in one of the large, leather seats. Sarah did the same. Once they were settled into their seats, Dr. Mychael turned to Sarah, her eyes darting along Sarah's face. "How are things?"

"They're okay. I haven't had anything else strange happen."

"Okay, good. I'm glad to hear that." Dr. Mychael shifted her weight to become more comfortable in her chair. "How are you feeling?"

"Still scared at times," Sarah admitted, "but I'm trying not to let it affect me too much."

"Okay, that's good but make sure you are in tune with your emotions and not pushing them away. Allow yourself to feel but just don't let the fear control."

"Easier said than done," Sarah responded, looking off into the distance.

"Absolutely. It's a hard balance." For several minutes they sat in silence thinking when the phone rang and startled them.

Sarah stood up and got the phone. This time, she gave it straight to Dr. Mychael who answered. Dr. Mychael was only a few sentences into the conversation when her face dropped. It held an expression Sarah had never seen. It was an expression somewhere between stunned and gravely saddened. Something was terribly wrong.

When she hung up, she looked over at Sarah, her face frozen and stunned. "There's been a terrible accident," she paused as though holding back emotions, "they don't know if he is going to make it."

"Who?"

"John."

CHAPTER THREE

LOCATION: CHAITI
TIME: PRESENT DAY

"I don't know what to think of you, Ajahadé," Jarah said in their native Chaitian as she took food from Ajahade's hand. "You always seem to know when I need some food for the children." The small, frail-looking skin stretched around her mouth to make a beautiful but sheepish smile.

"Oh, I know it must be hard for you and your husband to raise the boys, especially with the crops the way they have been lately. I figured since word was out that the market was stocked, I'd better get enough for both of us," Ajahadé replied as she followed Jarah deeper into the dirt hut.

The younger lady smiled back as she placed the food on the floor near the thin cloth they used as a table. "Sit down," she said, motioning toward the floor. "Sellen should be coming soon, but please get comfortable."

Ajahadé nodded her thanks as she folded her thin, but

strong body to the floor while Jarah did the same. Bending close, Jarah spoke, her voice a whisper, "Have you heard the news?"

Ajahadé nodded. "Yes, sounds like there is some stirring among the people over on the west side of the island."

"Yes," Jarah responded, "I think our people are finally upset about our repression."

Ajahadé nodded. "I can't blame them."

"Me either. It saddens me to think that my boys are probably going to grow up not knowing our Chaitian tongue."

"Are you not teaching it to them?"

"I was, but now I've stopped because the Jkika kept speaking Chaitian in public, and it got too dangerous."

Ajahadé nodded with understanding. "That's probably a good move, at least until they get old enough to understand the gravity of this situation."

"Aj," Jarah's voice was serious as she shifted to look Ajahadé in the eyes, "do you think it's possible this could break out into another war?"

Ajahadé looked serious for several minutes as she recalled precursory events to the last war—events that Jarah had been too young to experience—and the current situation. "Honestly, it's too early to tell, Jarah. We are just going to have to see."

Jarah nodded, a worried look on her young face. "Okay, you're right. We'll just have to see."

LOCATION: UNITED STATES OF AMERICA
TIME: PRESENT DAY, ONE MONTH AFTER THE ACCIDENT

The month after the accident was a whirlwind. Sarah watched as the woman who was always calm, cool, and collected transformed into a worried, restless grandmother. John's accident had occurred in Germany, and though his injuries were not quite as extensive as they had originally thought, it still was a week before he was able to be flown back to the United States for treatment. While he was now stable and conscious, the doctors said his legs had been so badly damaged that it would take a while for him to be able to walk normally again; they were still unsure whether there would be other lasting effects.

Dr. Mychael had maintained constant pulse on his condition through frequent telephone conversations. Now, it appeared that he would be flown to North Carolina so he could utilize the top medical facility in the state. Dr. Mychael was planning to see him and she asked Sarah to go with her.

"Sure," Sarah had responded. "When do you want to go?"

"He is on his way there now, so I've called my driver. We'll probably leave around 5. Will that work?"

"Yes," Sarah responded, swallowing at the fact that Dr. Mychael had her own personal chauffeur.

<><

"Here, you'll need this," Dr. Mychael said to Sarah about an hour later as they were preparing to leave.

"A hat?"

"Yes, do you not think it's nice? I have others...."

"No, no, this is fine," Sarah said, putting on the pink hat that matched her outfit perfectly. The front of the hat drooped down slightly in the front, almost covering her face; however, Sarah did not mind. *I wish I had had one of these when I was a teenager...this would have made me feel more invisible, just like I wanted.*

"Okay," Dr. Mychael responded, placing a hat on her own head and grabbing her sunglasses. She gave Sarah some as well; they both walked toward the front door. Outside sat a black Lincoln sedan with a man in a dark suit standing by it.

Putting on her sunglasses, Sarah followed Dr. Mychael out the front door and watched in amazement as the chauffeur opened the doors for both of them.

"Thank you, Tom," Dr. Mychael said as soon as all three were in the vehicle.

"Sure, no problem, Doc. I'm really sorry to hear about all his troubles. He's a good kid."

"Thank you," she said solemnly. "I'm sorry too. He's a strong one though."

"Absolutely," Tom responded as he guided the car down the long driveway. After about a half-hour, they turned onto a narrow road that looked like an entrance to a facility. "I'm taking you in the back way, Doc."

"Thank you, Tom. You know I appreciate that."

Tom smiled as he pulled up to a gate that read: "Authorized Personnel Only." He entered a code into the box outside the gate and waited for it to open. He drove the vehicle through them and followed the road toward a large hospital building. "I'm dropping you off here," he said. "Barry is going to take you the rest of the way."

Dr. Mychael nodded as Tom pulled to a stop. Instantly, Barry appeared and opened the doors for both women. He led them toward the building. After entering a code, he opened the door and led them inside.

After several minutes of walking, they arrived outside a hospital room door. Another suited man was standing outside. Barry nodded at the man turned to look at Dr. Mychael, his face serious.

"Look, Ma'am, I've been told to warn you that he's not in great shape. You may want to prepare yourself."

Dr. Mychael gently tapped Barry on the shoulder as she nodded. "I know. Thank you." She walked past him and opened the doors to the room.

<><

Inside the room lay a young man with his eyes closed and almost his entire body wrapped in a cast or bandages, including most of his face. Dr. Mychael calmly walked to the side of his bed. For a moment, she stood there silent, watching him like a caring mother watching her sleeping infant.

"John," she said quietly, "John, honey, its Grandmamma. I'm here."

Sarah watched as the young man's eyes slowly opened. For a moment, his blue eyes, which seemed strangely familiar, searched his grandmother's face as she spoke. "We made it here to see you, honey."

He murmured something indistinct.

"What is it, honey?" Dr. Mychael said, her voice sweet and gentle.

"Hey, Grandmamma," he responded very quietly. Sarah felt tears building up behind her eyes.

"Hi, honey," Dr. Mychael responded, swallowing back her own tears.

"W–where am I?"

"You're in North Carolina. They flew you here so that you can heal in private and do physical therapy here. It's quieter."

"D–did they–fol–" he paused, mid word, and let the sentence hang.

"I'm here with Sarah," Dr. Mychael said gently and waved Sarah over to the bedside.

"Hi," Sarah said, her voice very quiet.

"Hi," John responded, equally quietly. "I have heard about you."

Sarah felt a small smile teasing around her lips. "I hope good things."

"Yes," he said, his eyes drooping, "all good things."

At about that time, the nurse came in. "He is on heavy painkillers," the nurse said to Dr. Mychael. "They make him very drowsy, but we've got to keep his pain down."

Dr. Mychael nodded with understanding.

<><

The next few weeks were a blur for both Sarah and Dr. Mychael. While Sarah spent a lot of time at the retirement village and was not able to return to the hospital, she continued to check in with Dr. Mychael every day, either by physically stopping by the Mychael estate on her way home from work or by phone to see how she and John were doing. The stress of the whole situation was showing on Dr. Mychael, so Sarah insisted on helping with her tasks.

John was making progress. Today, they were going to remove all the bandages and the cast off his right arm. Tom had brought Sarah and Dr. Mychael to the ospital, and Barry walked them to John's room.

"How is he today, Barry?" Dr. Mychael asked as they entered the elevator.

"He's better, ma'am. He is awake and alert today and definitely ready to have some of the bandages removed."

Dr. Mychael nodded just as the elevator doors opened.

A few minutes later, they walked into the room. John was sitting up and he smiled as they walked in; all the bandages were removed from his face.

"Hi," he said cheerfully.

"Hi, honey," Dr. Mychael said as she walked over to his bedside. "How are you feeling?"

"Better. They removed a lot of the bandages and they are removing this cast in a little while." He motioned toward his right arm.

"Good. That will feel better."

John nodded. "Hi Sarah," he said, looking around Dr. Mychael to see Sarah standing behind.

Sarah started to walk toward his bed but stopped. For the first time, she got an unobstructed look at his face. She froze, shock washing over her as everything came flooding back. *The game, the church meeting, the letters! This guy is not* "John;" *this is **Chase**. Chase from so many years ago. How is it possible? I never thought I would see him again....*

"Are you okay, dear?" Dr. Mychael's gentle voice seeped through Sarah's thoughts and brought her back to the present.

She opened her mouth to say something, but no words came out; emotions and thoughts were flying inside her head at warp speed and creating a convoluted mass of thoughts she could not articulate. She cleared her throat. "Uh–um, I–I just need a moment," was all she managed to say as she slowly backed away from the bed.

"Okay, sweetie," Dr. Mychael said, exchanging a look with Barry who followed Sarah out of the room.

"I–I need some air," Sarah said to Barry as soon as they were outside the room.

"Sure, ma'am. Follow me." She followed him into the elevator and watched as he inserted a key into a keyhole on the elevator control panel and hit a button. A few minutes later, they reached the roof level of the hospital; he led her out onto the roof. "It isn't nice, but it's private."

"Thanks, Barry," Sarah said. He stayed by the door as she walked towards the edge, about six feet away, and sat down. *Wow. How is that even possible? How could Dr. Mychael's grandson be Chase? How could there possibly be a connection like that? How did I never put this together?*

Her mind flew. *But then again, I did meet him in South Carolina, so I guess this isn't all that far away. No, it is far! And the people here are so unconnected to those I grew up with–I came here because of that. I knew it was far enough away from Richard that I would know no one and no one would know me.*

Oh that man–Richard. The memories came flooding back. *Why did he have to discover our letters?* A cold shiver passed through her entire body as she recalled that dreadful afternoon when he had discovered her secret. Her mother had been away at work while Richard–who did not work on Fridays–had been home. He had walked into her bedroom, an envelope in his hand. On it, she could see Chase's handwriting.

Sarah felt her heartbeat and breathing increase as the memories came back. She saw the images of Richard: his angry face, his nostrils expanded and his eyes glaring with madness. His face was so angry she knew he was flipping to his evil side: the side that caused all logic, all reason or human consideration to fly away to a distant world. It was the side that turned him into a mean, cruel person with no mercy–a volcano of rage that exploded into hot, torturous lava that ate away at her flesh and burned her deeper and deeper. She remembered knowing that her life was in danger the moment he looked down at the letter and then back at her. He would not stop until he had inflicted enough pain to ease his evil heart.

But her ability to recall stopped at that point–it was as though it was blocked–but her body remembered. Her heart raced–she could feel it pounding in her chest–as another shiver flew down her spine, then another.

She could barely breathe. Her whole body trembled. She pulled her legs up into the fetal position and rocked herself back and forth. She knew it looked odd, but the motion of rocking somehow provided comfort; it always had. For several long minutes, she rocked back and forth on top of the roof as she tried desperately to find comfort from the panic filling her entire body. She rocked faster and faster until the comforting sensation gradually began to appear. The more it approached, the slower she rocked as she became calmer.

After some time, she stopped. She stayed in place for a

few long moments, her body tired. Then, she slowly looked up. Above her a small distance away stood Dr. Mychael, her caring eyes watching Sarah with concern and love. Sarah sat up and Dr. Mychael approached. For a moment, there was silence.

Sarah was the first to speak, her voice low and timid as she wiped her eyes with her hands. "How much of that did you see?"

Dr. Mychael slowly eased her older body down to sit on the roof beside Sarah. "Most of it, honey, most of it."

"And you didn't stop me?"

Dr. Mychael shook her head. "No, honey, you were already too far gone when I came up here; plus, you have to let those feelings out. The flashbacks are hard to handle because the feelings—and the terror—are real and your body responds to it." She paused. "But, dear, the threat is no longer here; it is just going to take time for your body to realize that. It won't realize it if I keep you from experiencing your feelings. Granted, some flashbacks are dangerous, so I won't let you go too far, but your body needs to realize that it's different now."

Sarah thought for several long moments. Dr. Mychael was right. The remembrance of that terror—of the pain, the helplessness, the defeat—was very hard to handle, and the physiological reaction was real and terrifying. But the threat was not real anymore. Richard was *not* here and he could not hurt her.

"You're right," Sarah said, her voice low. "Thank you."

"Sure, dear," Dr. Mychael responded, her soft voice comforting Sarah. For several minutes, they both sat in silence. Finally, Dr. Mychael spoke, "Do you have an idea what triggered the episode?"

"Yes," Sarah nodded. She took a deep breath before responding. "Do you remember the boy I told you about that I met one summer at a church function?"

"The nice one that you wrote letters to?" she asked.

"Yes, that one." Sarah paused. "Well, I believe that he is your grandson."

A look of surprise crossed the older lady's wrinkled face. "Oh my! That's incredible. How did we never put this together?"

"Well, you always called him John so—"

"Ah, yes," Dr. Mychael nodded. "That's his first name—which is what the family calls him—but he prefers to be called by his middle name, Chase. In fact, I think he's changed his legal name to Chase John Mychael instead of John Chase."

Sarah nodded. "That makes sense now."

Dr. Mychael smiled. "This is amazing—I'm so glad you two get to meet again after all these years!"

"Me too!" Sarah responded, finally seeing the happy part of the situation.

Then, Dr. Mychael grew serious. "What part triggered the

flashback? Did it bring back memories of your father?"

"Yes," Sarah responded, "and what happened when he discovered our secret letters."

Dr. Mychael paused before she responded, "Did you ever tell John what happened?"

Sarah shook her head. "No, my father watched me like a hawk after that, so I could never write another letter, let alone mail one. And then we moved. So there was really no way that Chase could find me after that."

Dr. Mychael nodded. "I see." For a few moments, the two women sat in silence as Sarah recovered from all that had just happened.

"Thanks for being here and not thinking I'm crazy," she said finally, her voice low and timid.

"Oh honey, you are not crazy—don't even think that. You have been through a lot. This is part of the process of healing and becoming stronger."

Sarah smiled timidly and swallowed back the emotions. "I appreciate that."

LOCATION: CHAITI
TIME: PRESENT DAY

The sun was about to dip below the horizon as Ajahade's bare feet quietly brushed over the dirt path in the once dense forest that was now brown. The farmers were still fighting hard to defend their diminishing crops from the fierce drought, but even more challenging was the unrest in the west side of the island. There had been rumors that the violence was growing in intensity and spreading eastward.

Today, she was walking the trail that led towards her brother's house. His dirt hut was part of the village that neighbored hers, but it was far enough from the other huts that it had significant privacy. Ishnomela, though a friendly and well-liked person, was one who appreciated privacy from the peering eyes of the Mashottiís—the primary group running the island now—while raising his Chaitian family.

She approached the hut and saw his two boys outside in the yard playing. They were tossing a rock—makeshift for a ball—back and forth. When they saw her approach, they instantly stopped and ran over.

"Aunt Aj!" they screamed and gave her big hugs. "So good to see you—what are you doing here?" the older one said as the younger interrupted, "Wanna play with us?"

"Sure! But let me say hi to your parents first, okay?"

"Okay," the little one nodded. "They're inside."

Ajahadé nodded and smiled at them again before walking towards the hut.

A few moments later, Ajahadé was inside the hut. "It is so good to see you!" the dark-skinned, petite mother said in French as she gave Ajahadé a hug. "Ish has been wondering how you have been. We went to your hut the other day, but you weren't there."

"Oh! I'm sorry I missed you," Ajahadé replied in French. "I've been going back and forth a lot helping some of the locals fare this drought."

"Getting food for them?"

"Yes, and helping them get water when we can."

"I see." The other lady paused. "We've been fortunate to find food pretty consistently. Our crops are so close to the river that it helps. Granted, the river is barely there now, but at least the soil isn't quite as dry."

"Makes sense—I just hope we get rain soon. This just can't go on much longer," Ajahadé responded just as her brother walked inside.

"Hi, Aj," he said, his dark weathered face stretching into a smile. "How are you?"

"Hi Ish. I'm okay. You?" She brought her gaze up to meet his, a Chaitian custom for those of higher ranking to do regardless of their gender—unlike the Mashottian tradition of restricting women from obtaining eye contact. Her tone of voice was enough for him to notice that something was bothering her.

"I'm fine." He looked at his wife. "Honey, would you mind checking on the kids? I'm not exactly sure what they are doing out there."

"Sure," she responded but passed him a knowing glance. "I'll give you guys some sibling time."

"Thanks, honey," he responded and she quietly left the clay hut.

"Aj," Ishnomela said and waited for her to look at him. For a moment, they exchanged a look—Ajahadé passed him the secret signal corresponding with a request she would not dare to verbalize. "Okay," he responded to her silent request, and within a few minutes, he was removing the cover on a secret trapdoor, well-hidden within their family hut.

Ajahadé went first. She slowly lowered her thin, muscular body down into the tunnel; Ishnomela followed and pulled the trapdoor closed behind them. They were now in complete darkness. For several long minutes, they crawled through the tight underground tunnel that went deeper and deeper. Neither said a word and their bodies were almost completely quiet as they crept through the darkness.

The tunnel took a right turn and then a sharp left. It descended deeper into the ground and made another right turn. Ajahadé paused and felt along the stone wall. Feeling an opening to her right, she pulled her body through and then stopped, knowing there was a slight drop off ahead. She felt along the base of the tunnel and located the edge. Then, she felt along the top and scoped out exactly the height of the tunnel. She slowly sat up—missing the tunnel ceiling by only a few inches—and then pushed her legs in front of her towards the edge.

Putting her hands on the edge, she used her arms to lower her body slowly down the edge until her feet hit solid ground. Ishnomela followed. A few moments later, she heard a match strike and a small flame began to lighten the underground room. Using the match, Ishnomela lit a small torch that was located in the corner and walked towards her. The light filled the room and revealed the many weapons that were stored there. "It's safe to talk now," he said in their native language, his voice quiet.

Ajahadé nodded in understanding but paused several moments before she spoke. "I heard rumors that the unrest is spreading east." Her voice was emotionless and strong as she spoke in Chaitian. "Have you had confirmation?"

"It is," Ishnomela responded his voice also void of emotion. "The fighting between the Mashottiís and Chaitians is increasing, and they have gone slightly east, but not much, yet. Only a few villages."

"Okay," Ajahadé responded. "What does the strength of the Chaitians look like?"

"Not much, but they are skillful. What they lack in might, they have in strategy."

"True Chaitian style," Ajahadé responded, a hint of pride in her voice. "What villages have been taken?"

"None so far, but I believe Jayha is about to fall to Mashottiís."

"Define *fall*," Ajahadé responded.

"Fall as in….well…some time ago, the Mashottiís started

taking Chaitian women and girls, turning them into sex slaves in the Palace. The Chaitians started fighting back to the Mashottiís to end the kidnappings. I think the Mashottiís were startled by the fact that the Chaitians fought back."

"Obviously," Ajahade's voice still had no emotion. "I mean, the Mashottiís have a lot of people–battle strength, as it were–and weapons. After the last war, the Chaitian people are now such a small number and they–we–have few to no weapons. It makes no battle-sense to go up against such a giant like the Mashottiís."

"But we are a strong and moral people. We love our families and we will not tolerate others–including the Mashottiís–hurting our women or little girls."

"Exactly," Ajahadé responded, the hint of pride returning. "So, the Mashottiís were startled. Then what?"

"They came back and have been using weapons against us. Our side is fighting a tough battle, outsmarting the Mashottiís and using the land to our advantage, but I don't think we can sustain it much longer."

"We need something more," Ajahadé responded, deep in thought. "We don't have strength or many good weapons; we could recruit people, which I imagine will be done soon, but we could never reach the same numbers as the Mashottiís. What we need is inside knowledge. We need to get the Mashottiís from the inside-out. "

"Agreed," Ishnomela responded. "But things aren't the way they used to be. We've lost top resources."

"I know," she responded, her voice somewhat distant as

she thought about the past.

"Look, Aj," Ishnomela continued, his voice serious and his eyes on her face; she brought her gaze up to his. "If this thing gets much worse, we're going to need you. I can't do this all on my own—you know what a big task it is."

Ajahadé nodded. "It is big and a lot rests on this but—" she shook her head. "I can't, Ish."

"But—"

"No!" Ajahadé said firmly, her voice rising with firmness and dipped in pain. "I just can't, Ish."

He swallowed hard and then shook his head. "I know, I know, sis." He paused. "But—if, and only if—this gets out of hand, please do promise me that you will at least think about it."

Ajahadé thought for several long moments before slowly nodding her head. "Okay."

CHAPTER FOUR

Sarah had approached that hospital room door before; however, this time she hesitated as her feelings were conflicted. She was happy to see Chase again, but she wondered if he remembered her. If he did, she wondered if he would hate her because she had dropped him so abruptly. She was scared he would not understand why she had stopped writing and yet happy that finally there would be no person—such as Richard—standing in between them.

Sarah felt a knot in her stomach as Barry led her toward Chase's room. Standing outside his door was a familiar guard. "They just finished," the guard said to Barry. Barry nodded; then he opened the door for Dr. Mychael and Sarah to enter.

The cast had been removed from Chase's right arm, and he sat up in bed watching TV. He turned to look at them as they entered. "Hi," he said and turned off the TV.

"Hi, honey," Dr. Mychael responded. "I'm hungry. I'm going to go down to the cafeteria to get some food. Do either of you want anything?"

"I can go down there for you," Sarah responded and started to move towards the door.

Dr. Mychael waved her hand. "Thanks, honey, but no. I need a walk."

"Okay," Sarah said and asked for a sandwich.

Dr. Mychael left the room. For a moment, there was silence between Sarah and Chase. She walked toward the window and stared outside as she searched for words to say. After several moments, she turned and looked over to see his gaze on her—he was looking at her face as though trying to read her emotions.

Then he spoke, his voice soft and gentle, "Do you remember…?"

She looked into his eyes only briefly before looking down. "Yes," her voice was equally quiet. "It was a hot day and—and we were so young."

A smile stretched across his injured face. "Yes, it sure was and—let's face it—that game was pretty lame."

She giggled and turned toward him. "Yeah, it was—it's no wonder we were bored by it." She walked to his bedside.

"Absolutely. I mean, talking about our music and our dreams was *so* much more exciting." He smiled. "Did you end up becoming an author and veterinarian?"

She shook her head. "No, but I did publish some poems."

"Seriously?"

"Yes, but it was through a penname, not my real one."

"Oh, I see. I was going to ask where because I've searched for you so many times."

Her face looked sad. *Aw, he searched for me.* She brought her gaze up to meet his. "I am sorry I cut off so abruptly. I–I did not want to."

His facial expression got serious as his beautiful blue eyes searched her face. "I figured it wasn't in your control." He paused, his voice getting even quieter. "Did *he* find out?"

She bit her bottom lip and slowly nodded, her gaze again on the floor.

"I'm so sorry." His voice was incredibly sad and apologetic. For a while, there was silence as though he was processing what he had heard or contemplating what to say next. After a while, he spoke, his voice inundated with concern, "Did he–did he hurt you?"

Again, she nodded.

She heard a rustling of the covers and looked up to see him shifting his position so that he could see her more clearly. "I am so sorry," he said gently. "I never meant for that to happen."

"I know you didn't," she responded, "and it wasn't your fault. The mailbox at that abandoned house collapsed or was stolen. Because the mailman knew where I lived, he put your letter in my home mailbox."

"I didn't think they were allowed to do that."

"They probably aren't, but he knew my family so he was probably just trying to be helpful. I'm just glad you didn't put a return address on it."

"Me, too, but–" he paused, "I am really very sorry about it all. It hurts me to know that something I did caused you harm."

"It wasn't your fault, Chase. It wasn't really anyone's fault but Richard's; his actions are his alone."

Chase nodded. "But still, knowing that I somehow aided or contributed to his outburst and angry rage bothers me."

"Well, it is in the past and I'm safe now, for the most part."

"What do you mean 'for the most part'?" His voice was concerned.

"To my knowledge, he doesn't know where I am."

Chase nodded. "Good. But I suspect he is looking." Sarah nodded. "I know we've probably talked about this before, but since he is your adopted dad, is there something legal you could do, like, with the adoption agency or something?"

Sarah shook her head. "No, not really. Since I'm an adult

now, the agency doesn't care. I could get a restraining order again but those are temporary and he has a tendency to escape before the police find him anyway."

Chase nodded. His eyes continued to show their concern. "Sarah, is there anything I can do to help you be safe? You can stay at Grandmamma's place–I have security there."

Sarah nodded. "Thank you. She's already told me I can stay with her if I need to."

"She means it, too. And her place is fenced and gated–as you know–and I can also easily up the security a notch."

"Thank you, Chase." Sarah paused for a moment as she looked around the room and then back to Chase's face. His bright blue eyes were full of so much concern that she struggled to find words. Instead, she decided to switch subjects. "Enough about me. How are you feeling?"

"I feel better now that my arm is free but I'm still sore." He wiggled his fingers. "My legs ache, which–at least I think–is a good sign. Means there's feeling in them."

"Good point." Sarah paused for a moment as she wondered what it could possibly feel like not to know how long it would take to walk easily again. "How are you holding up with all of this?" Sarah asked her voice soft and rich with sympathy.

He took a deep breath and shrugged his muscular shoulders. "It's kind of hard, but I'll be fine. Just not thinking about it too much and trying to focus on feeling better."

"Gotcha," Sarah responded, nodding. "Well, if anyone can

recover from all these injuries, you can."

Chase smiled and looked at her. His eyes landed on hers and for a moment, time stood still. Though time had taken its toll on both of them and life had changed them from the teenagers they were when they met so many years ago, she still felt the connection they had had then. It felt different—Sarah wasn't sure how—but it was still there.

<><

The day was bright and sunny and the air was crisp and clear as Sarah pulled herself onto the bare back of the horse. "Come on, Mum!" she shouted to the dark-haired, muscular-built woman on the horse beside her.

"Okay. Let's go!" Sarah's mother clicked to the horse and both animals galloped across the field. Over the hill and down the other side, the horses galloped until they reached the woods. There, they slowed down and followed a long path before finally reaching an opening to the shoreline.

They walked onto the beach and stopped several feet from the water. Sarah and her mother dismounted and sat down on the white sand. For a while they simply enjoyed the gentle sounds of the waves lapping up onto the shore and the seagulls squawking from the trees.

"Listen to nature," Sarah heard her mother say, "listen to them—the birds, the water, the trees; they all have a message for you. They will quietly tell you when everything is okay or when something bad is about to happen. But you have to be still and listen, or you will not hear."

Sarah nodded and stayed still to listen. She heard the

gentle breeze flowing through the trees and saw dolphins splashing in the water, but she could not understand the message—she had never been able to understand despite her mother always reminding her there were messages.

Then an unusual sound broke the moment: it was the sound of a dog barking in the distance. The sound came closer and closer until a big black dog appeared and began licking Sarah's face.

"Zeus!" Sarah said quickly as she opened her eyes and realized everything had just been a dream. "What is it, buddy? I was sleeping!" The dog jumped off the bed and began pacing back and forth in the room. *Eh,* Sarah moaned as she dragged her body out of the bed, *he has to go outside.*

Once outside, she let Zeus run loose without a leash, but she kept him in her sight. For a moment, she paused to listen to nature. She heard the crickets chirping from the woods but something felt slightly off. *It is not much...just something seems a little strange tonight. What could it be?* She stayed quiet listening for nature's message and hoping to decipher it. But she could not. After a while, she called Zeus and walked back inside the house.

The experience left her perplexed; so much so that—despite going back to bed—sleep was nowhere to be found. She got up and went into the living room. Turning on the TV, she listened to the early morning news. *Just the normal chaos,* she thought, as she walked toward the kitchen to get some water.

"Recently, there have been rumors of conflicts in several island nations," she heard the TV announcer say. *"Experts believe the conflicts started due to competition for fresh*

water and farming supplies. While these nations are surrounded by water, they lack the technology or capacity to turn sea water into fresh water and so they are losing crops by the minute. This is causing increasing tension between the native people and other groups in the islands."

Sarah finished pouring the water and went back to watch the rest of the news segment, but it had already shifted to Hollywood: *"Word is that singer CJ is taking a hiatus. No word yet on why he has chosen to do this."*

"Hm, interesting," Sarah said out loud as she began thinking about the singer. "It is not like him to take breaks, but he has been quite busy with albums and appearances lately. It is probably a good thing for him to slow down a bit."

Zeus walked over and put his huge black head on her knee. Gently, she stroked his hair as her mind darted from one topic to another before finally settling down to think about Chase. He was doing significantly better and the doctors were anticipating that he would be able to go home tomorrow. He was planning to go to Dr. Mychael's house to stay until he finished physical therapy. Though Sarah was saddened that he would need so much physical therapy, she was happy that she would get to see him a while longer.

She had gone to the hospital with Dr. Mychael several times a week for the last two months, but the two of them had not had a spare moment to themselves. Though Chase had made it clear that he appreciated her visiting and there had been moments of eye contact that made something within her chest jump, she did not know what he was thinking or anything more about his feelings for her.

Her heart was hopeful that the foundation they had built as teenagers could make things the same today, but her logical side told her that time could change things. They were not the same as they were before—in fact, she had no idea whether he had a girlfriend, what had transpired in his life the years they had lost contact, or what he *actually* did for a living. There were so many questions and—without time alone—no real answers.

"Only time and patience will let me learn more," she thought aloud. "I will learn these answers after I have more time with him." Though she knew this, something within her wanted to skip ahead to see if there would still be a spark between them after they got to know each other more. Would he still like her?

LOCATION: UNITED SATES OF AMERICA
TIME: THE NEXT DAY

The sun shone brightly as Sarah watched the dark, black SUV approach the gate to the Mychael estate. A smile stretched across her face as she opened the front door and walked down the stone steps to greet them.

"Hi, Sarah," Dr. Mychael said from the other side of the vehicle.

"Good morning!" Sarah responded and then watched as Tom opened the back door and revealed Chase sitting in the back seat. His bright blue eyes met hers, and for a moment, both of them paused. She felt her heart jump within her chest.

"Hi," he said quietly.

"Hi, Chase," Sarah responded equally quiet, just as Tom stepped in between them to help Chase stand up. Bruce appeared with a wheelchair and Chase sat down.

A few minutes later they were inside the house. "Wow, that smells amazing," Chase said, as Sarah removed homemade cinnamon rolls from the oven.

"And they are just as good as they smell," Dr. Mychael said as she prepared the tea.

Sarah felt her face growing warm. "I hope so. I don't use a recipe, so it is always a bit of a gamble."

"Those are usually the best kind," Chase responded. "Are you sure there is nothing I can do to help?"

Both women waved their hands. "No, we are good. Thank

you though. It'll be done in just a moment."

A few minutes later, the tea and cinnamon rolls were on the porch table waiting. "You two go ahead and start eating; I'll be back in a little while," Dr. Mychael said, leaving Sarah and Chase alone on the stone porch.

"Sarah," Chase said, once Dr. Mychael was gone, "I have been thinking about all that you have done for our family. I really hope you know how much we appreciate it."

"Oh," Sarah shrugged, "it's nothing."

"No, it really isn't nothing," Chase said and then realized the strange wording of his sentence. "Sorry for the double negative there, but honestly, what you've done *is* something and it is important to us. All the time you've spent making sure Grandmamma is okay and how you check on her regularly. That alone means a lot to me—especially since I travel so much and can't always be here."

"She is a wonderful person; I love to be around her."

Chase nodded. "She is. And it also means a lot to me how you came to the hospital to see me."

"Of course," Sarah said. "I wanted to make sure you were okay."

Chase smiled. "I will be."

"Yes, for sure."

LOCATION: CHAITI
TIME: PRESENT DAY

The darkness was deeper than the depth of space—no light from the moon or stars was able to fight against it. Ajahadé heard footsteps. Slowly, she slid out of bed and walked through the doorway into the hall, her bare feet making no sound on the wood floor.

Finally, a small window allowed the moon to fight against the darkness and a few slivers of its light entered the hallway—just enough light to allow Ajahadé to spot something move in the shadows. A dark man, his huge figure covering most of the hallway, crept ahead. He turned to the left for only a moment and something sparkled in his hand. It was something shiny, perhaps metal. *A knife,* she thought.

She followed him. He turned and entered the children's bedroom. *NO!* Ajahadé screamed internally. *Don't hurt them!*

Without a single thought for her own safety, she sprang forward and burst into the bedroom just as he reached the bed of the sleeping little girl. His knife in his left hand, he turned to look at Ajahadé, an evil smile on his lips. Before she could reach him, he turned, grabbed the girl by her neck, drew his knife up to her throat, and swiped it across. Blood gushed out.

Suddenly, the entire scene vanished from Ajahade's sight. She woke up.

Shivering from head to toe, Ajahadé almost sprang up in bed but stopped. *Where am I?* she thought as she felt around her. Feeling the familiar bedding beneath her and then the dirt floor beside her, she took a breath. *I'm at home. I'm safe.* She sat up.

But the feelings inside whirled around like a tornado. The images...the thoughts...the memories came back. She saw the little girl, her dark curly hair bouncing in the wind and her beautiful brown eyes laughing as she ran across the fields...she saw a little boy splashing in the water...and then she saw a cruel man with a dagger and an evil plan...she felt the pain, the agony, the helplessness of that night—so many years ago—that would forever be sketched in her memory. True, the dream had not been real or a precise depiction of what had happened; however, the terror and the feelings were real. And the memories were so horrible Ajahadé wished they had been only dreams.

Rubbing her own neck, she felt the raised skin of her scars and followed her neckline to the necklace that hung there. She felt the heart-shaped charm and gently held it closer to her chest. Though many years had passed and times had gotten bad with the drought, Ajahadé had never considered selling it; instead, it always had remained on her neck—she had not taken it off, except for repair, in over a decade.

Today, she held it close as the memories came back. *The Mashottiis are cruel people,* she thought. *They should not have won that war and they cannot win this battle.*

But fear gripped her. *I cannot have that happen again...anyone close to me can be a target, and I have people close to me even now.* She shivered at the thought.

Though it was still night, she knew that sleep was nowhere to be found. She slipped out of bed and opened the trapdoor for the tunnel beneath her hut. Crawling through the tunnel, much like the one in Ishnomela's house, she took several twists and turns before finally reaching an opening underground. Lighting a torch, she waited for the flames to light up the room before she started moving. She walked around the periphery of the room to ensure that nothing had changed.

Once assured that everything was exactly as she had left it, Ajahadé walked over to the two large punching bags suspended from the ceiling of the cave. With fierce skill and accuracy, her hand flew toward her target with incredible force, never missing while her muscular legs pounded the bags with greater strength than anyone would imagine given her small stature. She punched and kicked the bags over and over again, ignoring any hint of pain. Time stretched on, but Ajahadé did not slow down. With determination, she continued practicing, cultivating the strength that had been buried for too long and preparing for a fight that would soon come.

LOCATION: UNITED STATES OF AMERICA
TIME: PRESENT DAY, THREE DAYS AFTER HOSPITAL
DISCHARGE

"Are you *sure* you don't need any help with dinner?" Sarah asked Dr. Mychael for the second time.

"No, honey, I've got this. Thank you, though," Dr. Mychael said from the kitchen. "You just go relax in the library or somewhere, and I'll let you know when it's ready."

"Okay," Sarah responded and walked down the hall to the library. Even though nothing in the room had changed in several months, the room always fascinated her. Its dim lighting, international artwork and collectables, and extensive literature from around the world made her feel more at ease. It was almost as though the room—with its diversity—made her remember her freedom of culture. She wasn't bound to the American culture or way; she had the freedom to be different—just like all the different pieces within those walls and the cultures they represented.

Today, she slipped quietly into the room and scanned the shelves. Each book had been placed neatly and carefully in alphabetical order on the dark oak bookshelves. Some of the books looked old—almost as though they were bought and kept for historical purposes. Her eyes scanned the titles—they were mostly books on countries, politics, medicine, psychology, sociology, and cultures. Her eyes landed on one title in a foreign language, and she paused at the familiarity. The images of an island nation on the front looked similar to home. She was instantly curious and reached to pull it off the shelf, just as she heard the door open.

Turning, she saw crutches entering the room.

"Hi," Chase said as he got closer, his voice quiet. "Finding anything interesting?"

"I find this whole room interesting," Sarah said, her eyes surveying the room. "Its diversity makes me feel…" She let the sentence hang as she searched for words.

"Like you can be yourself in here? Like you're not bound to the dominate culture but can be yourself with your native culture?" He hobbled over to the leather chair and sat down.

Sarah looked at him, a look of perplexity on her face. "Yes, that is it exactly. How did you know?"

"Because I put myself in your shoes as much as I could. I mean, coming to this country and having to conform to our way of life—our busy way of life—and being forced into such a conservative culture for most of it," he paused, "well, it must have been constraining."

She nodded. "It was."

"And I also know how I feel when I go to different countries. I appreciate their cultures and I'm fascinated by their ways of life, but on the other hand, I feel like a giraffe in a herd of cattle. I just know I stick out."

She smiled. "I like that analogy."

A sneaky smile danced around his lips. "I'm glad because I just made it up on the spot. Aren't ya proud? Does it make me creative?"

"Hm…" Sarah responded, putting her pointer finger up to her lips, "I'd say you get one point for creativity."

"*One* point? Only one?" he asked, smiling. "It's gotta be more than that!"

She smiled back. "Okay, two points for creativity."

He smiled. "Okay, I'll accept that."

"But seriously, thanks for understanding. It can be difficult sometimes with the whole cultural differences."

"Do you ever miss home?"

She nodded. "Yes. I mean, I know I was young when I left, but that it is still part of who I am—it is where I came from, so I know it affects me."

"Yeah, that makes sense. Have you ever thought about going back?"

"Yeah, I've thought about it. But—but I just can't." Her voice trailed off.

Chase's caring eyes gently watched her face until she looked up at him. Without saying a word, she knew exactly what his light blue eyes were saying to her: *I care about you, Sarah, and I know why you can't go back. I understand and sympathize.* For several long moments, they kept each other's gaze until finally

Sarah spoke, "Do you ever get to go back to see your family?"

Sadness crossed his face for several moments before he responded, "No. After you and I broke contact, everything got worse with my parents. They stopped supporting the idea of making music my career and kept trying to push me towards computer science, which in hindsight, I understand." He paused. "It is more practical. But I don't have that kind of mind. Never have and never will."

"That's okay. You do not have to be in computer science to succeed."

"True, but they didn't see it that way. And when I dropped out of college, they kinda lost it. I would contact them but they stopped responding to me. It was almost as if I were dead to them."

"Are you serious?"

He nodded.

"That is awful, Chase. I'm so sorry."

"Thanks," he responded, his voice still low with sadness. "But it's okay. It's in the past now."

Sarah looked thoughtful. "Does Dr. Mychael ever talk about them?"

"Some. I know that things got worse between my parents and they separated. I don't know what happened to my mom but my dad is still working at the same place and seems to be doing okay."

"Gotcha," Sarah responded. "I'm sorry to hear that too."

Chase shrugged. "It's okay. I mean, it may be for the better–they didn't really get along."

Sarah nodded. At just that time, they heard Dr. Mychael calling from the kitchen.

"It looks like the food is ready," Chase said, smiling. "Let's go enjoy this chicken."

LOCATION: UNITED STATES OF AMERICA
TIME: PRESENT DAY, THREE MONTHS AFTER ACCIDENT

The fiery rays of the sun glared down on Sarah as she and Zeus walked through the woods at a nearby park. A cool breeze whipped around her face as she followed the dirt path. *My feet are too constrained,* she thought. She bent down and took off her running shoes and then continued down the dirt path. The pebbles and stones along the path massaged her tired feet as she walked.

Up ahead of them were huge boulders overlooking a large pond; she reached down, unhooked Zeus from his leash, and let him roam about while she climbed up onto the rock. For several long minutes, she soaked up the sunshine. She closed her eyes and thought about Chase—how injured he had been but how he had already made so much progress. She thought about his demeanor—it was sincere and genuine—and how warm and calm she felt when around him. She wondered what he did for a living, and she also wondered why his voice sounded so familiar. True, she'd heard it as a teenager, but it was very similar to another voice she had heard more recently. Even still, it was his character that she liked the most. He seemed genuine, and she felt a sense of warmth every time he looked at her.

She heard a small rustling sound near the rock. Looking down, she saw Zeus sniffing around in the leaves. He jerked his head up and looked across the pond. Following his gaze, Sarah noticed a young lady walking on the other side of the pond with a Scottish terrier at her feet. *That is a full-blooded Scottish terrier—maybe even show quality—looking at its build,* she thought as a knot appeared in her stomach. *You never see dogs like that around here—no one can afford them—you only see mixes and working dogs.* She took a better look at the woman and things began to make sense. *I think I have seen her before...*The knot in her stomach grew until it was a full-blown shiver. *Is this happening again? Have his people found me?*

As the fear grew, she fought it with logic. *This is a small town, so maybe you just bumped into her in town and it is nothing to worry about. But the dog. No one around here can afford a pedigree dog like that and—if they could—they would get a lab or another kind of dog that would actually help them. It more likely someone who is not from here but wanted to blend in....*

"Zeus, come," she said quietly. The huge dog—now many feet away—perked up his ears and ran over to her. She slid off the rock, put on his leash, and vanished into the woods.

CHAPTER FIVE

The night was dark despite the half-moon as Sarah walked Zeus around her neighborhood the next night. Walking slowly on the familiar path, Sarah's bare feet moved over the rocks along the path with familiarity. The crickets and tree frogs were beginning their soothing sounds while fireflies flashed their lights.

But a strange feeling appeared: she felt as though she were being watched. She looked around in every direction but saw no one in the darkness—even Zeus trotted along as though nothing out of the ordinary was happening. She stopped to listen, but no unusual noise could be heard.

The feeling grew. It hovered over her like a dark bird hovering above an innocent rabbit. *I can't take this anymore. I've got to get to the light—inside.* Turning back toward home prematurely, she called Zeus. He looked at her strangely—they were turning back a lot sooner than they normally did—but then complied.

The feeling grew even stronger. Sarah wanted to run to safety quickly, but she knew if someone was really watching her, running would make matters worse. It would cue the watcher that she knew she was being watched; this could cause him to close in on her faster. Instead, she quickened her pace just fast enough not to be obvious but still to help her get to safety faster.

Once inside her house, she immediately fastened all locks—including the bar lock on her front door—and checked all the windows to make sure they were locked and the curtains were closed. Still unsettled, she walked through every room of her small house, checking inside the closets, underneath the beds, and in any other place a small person could fit. *"It is just a feeling; no one is out there,"* Sarah said to herself. *"Nothing is here."*

She paced for several moments before walking to her bedroom closet. Pulling down a small box, she set it on the floor. Unlocking it, she pulled out a dark blue file folder filled with pictures and a few papers. Taking out the pictures, she looked at each one as the memories came back. It had been so hard to capture these pictures without letting the subjects know they were getting their pictures taken; however, it was worth the hassle to have these images. They were images of the people Richard had sent after her. Though some were only side-shots and others were blurry, they did their job of keeping her memories of their faces fresh in her mind.

What people she had not captured in the images were

described, in detail, on the pages within the folder. Reading each description again, she realized that none of them sounded like the girl she had seen at the park with the Scottish terrier. *So, either I never actually saw her before or she is a new one.*

Then she pulled out another piece of paper. On this paper was a list of license plates she had seen repeatedly back when Richard had almost found her. *I've got to remember these,* she thought as she studied each number. After several long minutes, she put all of the pages and pictures back into the folder.

Reaching into the box again, she pulled out a CD. Standing up, she reached for her laptop and put the CD into the drive. A few minutes later, a familiar sound of the song "You Are Gone" by CJ rose into the air like a majestic eagle souring through mountains and yet, like the arms of a loving husband, the familiar voice wrapped around her terrified heart and soothed it in ways words could not express. As it always did, the sound of CJ's voice calmed her nerves and made her feel more peaceful.

She sat back down near the box and pulled out an even smaller box. Inside lay a delicate necklace with a heart-shaped charm. Picking it up, she gently turned over the charm to reveal the symbol engraved on the back—the symbol, unlike anything seen in the United States, was native to her country. Gently, she rubbed her finger over the symbol as feelings of warmth, love, and loss washed over her. Images of times past flashed before her eyes and with them, a deep-rooted longing. *I miss her so much. She was the one person who truly loved me with all her heart,* she thought as she fought back the emotions, *and I don't even know if she is alive.*

LOCATION: CHAITI
TIME: PRESENT DAY

The sun was shining brightly as Ajahadé walked down the dirt road between some huts and toward the market. She approached a large table that held two baskets with only a few meager pieces of fruit in them. She eyed the bruised fruit, and then surveyed her surroundings.

Her eyes darted around and settled on one man who stood among the crowd. Instantly, her mind filled with recognition though her face showed no change. *Najandé,* Ajahadé thought as she made herself look back at the fruit and examine several of the oranges. *Why is he in this part of the country? This isn't his village.* Glancing back up, she saw him paying for some food several tables down. Quickly, she gathered her goods and paid the man behind the table.

Though her stride appeared to be casual and leisurely, her eyes darted back toward Najandé as he slowly walked away from the tables and the crowd. Ajahadé approached another table and began looking at the food there; however, her eyes darted back to the man. *Why is a Mashottii here? And where is he going?* He gradually walked farther away from the busy market toward the trees. A dark and mysterious feeling crept into Ajahade's body when she realized it was critical that she watch this man.

She walked away from the market and toward the village huts that were closest to the woods. Once out of site of the villagers, she took a sharp turn between the huts and walked back toward the woods. She followed

Najandé into the woods.

Her bare feet crept silently across the dirt as she dodged the brown forest foliage, her eyes keenly set upon Najandé as he moved through the forest seemingly unaware of her presence. He took one turn and then another. After only a short period of time, he entered a clearing. Though she desperately wanted to follow, there was no way to do so without being seen. She stopped and watched as he disappeared into the woods on the other side of the clearing.

Turning back, Ajahadé began walking toward Jarah's home. She climbed up the hill. When Jarah's hut came into sight, Ajahade's heart fell to the ground. Something was *terribly* wrong.

The area around Jarah's hut was deathly silent. None of her boys were outside, and the wood roof on the hut was completely gone—burned perhaps—and the entire area empty. *No!* Ajahadé cried inside as her heart sank even further. *The Mashottiís—they've been here!*

Putting the fruit underneath a dead bush, Ajahadé reached under her dress and grabbed the large knife that was always strapped to her leg.

Her senses on high alert and her footsteps quiet, she slowly crept toward the hut. Feeling along the outside wall of the hut, she stopped just out of sight of the door. She waited, listening for any sound of life, any movement, or any indication that the Mashottiís were still there.

The only sound she could hear was a small, almost

muffled, high-pitched sound, human yet indistinguishable. She stayed still and listened. After several moments, she realized it was the sound of muffled sobbing. Creeping forward, she approached the doorway. With knife in hand, she rounded the corner, ready for a fight.

But no one was there to fight her. Instead, she saw Jarah lying on the floor, holding her lower stomach. Her face was on the ground, buried flat into a pillow, but the sobs could still be heard. Ajahadé surveyed the room and saw the baby lying in the corner—completely still and silent. Unsure whether he was dead or alive, Ajahadé knew she must first attend to Jarah.

Letting her hand with the knife fall to her side, she spoke with a calm and gentle voice, "Jarah?" But her friend did not move. "Jarah, it's me—Ajahadé. Are you hurt badly?"

The pale woman slowly looked up. Her white face was badly bruised and her eyes were so swollen they were barely visible; her expression was clearly stunned. "It's me, Aj," Ajahadé repeated, and a look of recognition slowly spread over the other woman's face.

"Oh, Aj, it's you." Fresh tears poured out of her eyes, "It's you."

"Yes," Ajahadé responded still tense as her eyes continued to rove the room and outside the door. "Are you alone?"

The pale woman nodded. "Just the baby and me." Ajahadé nodded and walked over to join Jarah on the floor, her gaze still constantly darting back to the doorway. "Can you walk?"

The other lady still looked stunned. "Th–they came" she stuttered. "Th–they took my husband and my boys–all of them."

A look of sympathy washed over Ajahade's face, but then her face went expressionless again. "Jarah, I need you to focus. We've got to get you out of here. Are you able to walk?"

Tears still streaming down her bruised face, she slowly nodded. "Yes."

"Okay. Let's get you up." Ajahadé bent over to help Jarah to her feet, placing her hands on Jarah's shoulders.

"No! Don't touch me!" Jarah said and jerked back, then wrenched over in pain.

"Okay," Ajahadé said calmly. "I won't touch you anymore. But I'm putting my hand out here, and you can grab it if you need to, okay?"

Jarah nodded and struggled to her feet. Holding Ajahade's hand, she slowly stumbled a few steps and then stopped. "The baby, Aj, get my baby first. I will be okay."

"Let me get you to the wall first so you can lean against it," Ajahadé responded, helping Jarah hobble to the side of the hut. Once she was propped against the wall, Ajahadé put her knife back into its sheath on her leg and walked over to the baby.

The baby was still. Slowly, Ajahadé picked him up and held him in the crook of her arm; his body flopped lifelessly. Putting her hand on his chest, she felt no heartbeat; she heard no breathing. Checking everywhere she could think of for his pulse, she realized the traumatic truth: Jarah's baby boy was dead. *I can't tell her now—she'll give up, and I have to get her to safety.*

Walking back over to Jarah, she spoke, "Okay, let's go." Ajahadé put out her hand.

"But my baby..."

"I will come right back for him. We have to get you to safety first, and I'm not sure you can walk the whole way. I can't carry you both."

Jarah opened her mouth to protest but she could tell that Ajahadé was not going to budge. It was not a fight she could win. Instead, she held Ajahade's hand and let her help her to hobble slowly out of the hut.

Each step an extreme level of labor and pain, Jarah stumbled up the small hill near her house and stopped. "I–I can't."

"You've got to, Jarah. They are probably on their way back now to finish what they've started—we've got to get out of here." Ajahadé paused.

Jarah slowly put her right foot forward. "Ah!" she screamed. "It hurts!"

Ajahadé quickly looked around them to see if the scream had been heard and quietly responded, "I know, Jarah, I know."

Putting her left foot forward, Jarah clinched her teeth in pain. Then she took another step, and slowly another. Soon they were almost up the hill. "Almost to the top; we're almost there and then it's downhill."

Jarah nodded as fresh tears came streaming down. Then, suddenly she let out another scream and collapsed. Ajahadé barely caught her.

Ajahadé pulled Jarah's chest closer to hers—in a hugging position—then pulled Jarah's left arm across her own right shoulder. Kneeling down, Ajahadé allowed Jarah's body to flop across her shoulder and back. Then, after securing Jarah's arm across her own chest, she stood up.

Carrying Jarah across her shoulder, Ajahadé climbed up the rest of the hill and then down. She took a turn and then climbed another hill. Struggling under the weight, she descended the hill and saw a familiar sight appear before her eyes: Ishonomela's hut, with the oldest son outside chopping wood.

Looking up, he saw Ajahadé approaching. Instantly, he put down the ax and ran to her side. "Aunt Aj, let me help you," he said. Ajahadé nodded and let him help her carry Jarah's limp body the rest of the way to Ishnomela's home.

Once inside, Ishnomela —a former military nurse—sprang

into action. Within a few minutes, Jarah was cleaned, examined, bandaged, and laid on a bed to recover. "We've got to make sure she drinks some more. It's important that she stay hydrated," he whispered to Ajahadé and his wife, who both nodded. "Honey, Aj and I will be back in a minute; are you okay with watching her?" After the shorter woman nodded, the two siblings left.

Once inside the underground cave, Ishnomela spoke, "I'm assuming the Mashottiís got her?"

Ajahadé nodded. "Yes, she was in too much shock when I got there, so I didn't get any details, but it was their MO. They took everyone but Jarah and killed the baby."

Ishnomela cringed in sympathy. "How?"

"Suffocation, I believe," Ajahadé said, her voice matter-of-fact. "He had no cut marks but was not breathing. I suspect they suffocated him with a pillow or other such object."

Ishnomela stayed silent for a moment before his spoke, his voice low, "Does Jarah know?"

Ajahadé shook her head. "No, I did not tell her because I knew it would cause her to give up, and I didn't want that."

"What did you tell her?"

"That I'd go back for the baby—and I will—but just so she has closure. He was already gone."

Ishnomela nodded and for a moment, both siblings stayed silent as they processed what had just happened. Then, Ishnomela spoke, his voice low and troubled, "Aj, my sources have told me that the Mashottiís have gained more ground."

"How much more?" Ajahade's voice was still emotionless.

"They've seized Jayha," Ishnomela responded and Ajahadé nodded, her face barely showing her concern.

"Look, Aj," Ishnomela said and waited for her to look up at him, "Look, I know you want to stay out of it, but this is big. There is much violence and we—and all those connected to us—are targets."

Ajahadé responded, her voice showing sympathy, "I know, and Jarah is just one of many."

"Yes," Ishnomela said, then continued, his voice growing firm, "and staying out of it is not going to stop them. I need your help. Only with your help and your connections can these scumbags be taken down."

Ajahadé shook her head. "I can't, Ish." He opened his mouth to protest but she continued, "I can't. Innocent lives—" she paused as her voice grew with emotion, "innocent lives died because of me and I cannot—I *will* not—let that happen again."

"No," Ishnomela responded, his voice growing with even more firmness, "innocent lives died because of the Mashottiís. *They* are evil and *they* did it—not you. Do not put their actions on yourself."

Ajahadé shook her head and looked away from his gaze. "You don't understand."

"Look at me," Ishnomela responded and she complied. He then continued, his voice growing in anger, "You're right. I don't understand. I do not understand why my sister—who was one of the most influential people, best strategists and advisors within the Chaitian government—can just stand here while her people—our people and the very people she took an oath to defend—are being slaughtered, molested, and tortured!" His voice was now trembling with anger. "Jarah—your close friend—was raped and beaten. Her baby was killed and her entire family kidnapped by those scumbags and you do nothing!"

Ajahade's face flashed hurt and pain then tight with controlled anger. "Look," she paused and then continued, her voice low and strong. "I love our people, and I love you, Ish. I hate seeing the people I've worked so hard to keep safe be hurt and killed just as much as you do, if not more. But—" she paused and then continued between clinched teeth, her anger apparent but controlled, "until you experience seeing the ones you love with your whole heart being slaughtered ruthlessly before your own eyes while you stand there helpless and unable to defend them, do not—I repeat, do *not*—judge me." She turned and disappeared into the darkness.

LOCATION: UNITED STATES OF AMERICA
TIME: PRESENT DAY

"Wow, this band is really good, Sarah," an older lady with a wrinkled smile said as she sat next to Sarah in a large room within the Carolina Retirement Village. The bluegrass band had been playing for several songs and the crowd of senior citizens kept growing larger and larger.

"I'm glad you like them," Sarah said with a smile. "It was a bit of a challenge to get them to come."

"I bet! Not too many people wanna play for us old folks, but I'm glad you got 'em to come. They're real good."

"Hey honey," another older woman said from her wheelchair nearby, "I'm outta cola—would ya mind gettin' some for me?"

"Sure," Sarah responded and stood up. "I'll be right back." She walked to the other side of the room and noticed the refreshments were all gone. *I'll go get some from the kitchen.* Exiting the room, she walked down the long hallway and towards the kitchen.

She entered the kitchen and walked towards the pantry. "Oh hi, Sarah," a young man said from the back doorway.

Sarah saw him standing next to the door with a hand-truck full of sodas. "Hi Brad, how are you?"

"I'm good now that I've seen ya," he winked.

Oh man, Brad, just be quiet. "What are you doing? Refilling the colas?"

"Yep, I hear ya'll are out."

"Yeah, the Activity Room is completely out, so I was coming here to rob the pantry."

"Oh, that's no problem. I'll take these down there."

"Thanks, Brad,"

"Sure thing! Wanna join me?"

"Thanks, but I've got to go check on Mr. Two. He was not at the concert, so I want to make sure he is okay."

Brad looked at her with a teasing smile across his lips. "Sounds like an excuse to me."

"It isn't," Sarah responded.

"Uh-huh, sure. That's what ya always say." He turned towards the door and took a step forward. "One of these days—I tell ya—one of these days, I am gonna convince ya to go out with me."

Sarah simply smiled and walked away. *That's not going to happen.*

LOCATION: UNITED STATES OF AMERICA
TIME: SEVERAL DAYS LATER

The sun was shining in the cloudless sky as it slowly began its decent to the horizon. Birds were singing in the trees while several rabbits and squirrels scurried around Dr. Mychael's flower garden.

Sarah sat outside on the patio, quietly sipping her tea as she gazed off into the distance. There was so much to think about. *If* the lady at the pond had, in fact, been someone sent by Richard, then she knew it was only a matter of time before others would appear. She would start seeing the same people at random places—from the grocery store to the dog park. She imagined they would be collecting her information, her patterns, and habits and then—once they had enough—they would report it back to Richard. He would then conceive and execute his plan for her demise.

I have to stop it before it gets too far, but I can't just run now without confirmation, or—at the very least—more information in either direction. So far, all I have is a woman walking a pedigree dog and who looked vaguely familiar and a feeling of being watched—neither of these is enough to warrant me leaving. I need to see if this is just a hunch or if it is really a threat. Nevertheless, it takes time to plan an escape, so it does not hurt to start the process now. I already have all my bills on auto-pay from that account, so I have very little mail. I also have my bills being paid in my absence. I've withdrawn cash from my account every month and have a good stash of cash available, but I need to get some more—not a lot more, because too large of a withdrawal would be suspicious, but enough to add to my current cash stash....

"Sarah?" a quiet voice said from behind her. She looked up to see Chase walking up slowly. His leg was still in a cast, but he was not using crutches. "Would you care to have some company?"

"Sure," she said and used her foot to push the opposing chair out from underneath the table.

He sat down. "Thanks."

"Sure. Do you want some tea, too?"

"I'm okay. Thank you, though." For a moment there was silence as they both enjoyed the gradually fading sunshine. "It's so nice out here."

"Yeah, it really is," she replied. "It's so calm and peaceful."

He nodded. "It sure is."

"So, I know things have been busy and we haven't had too much time to talk, but what all happened in your life after we stopped, you know, sending letters?"

He sighed. "Wow, a lot has happened—I don't even know where to start."

"Hm, anywhere, Chase. I'm curious about it all."

He grinned. "Okay," he thought for a moment and then began, "Well, after we stopped, my family moved to Northern Virginia."

"How was that?"

"It was okay. The people were different—they had more northern-like mentality—but the schools had more programs, so it helped with my music."

"In what way were they different?"

"They just didn't have Southern hospitality—and they were very straight and to the point."

Sarah nodded in understanding. "That's kind of how Philly was as well. Was it a faster pace?"

"Yes, for sure. Definitely not the laid-back culture I was used to. But I adjusted and I'm glad now because I can handle a fast-paced environment."

"That makes sense. I kind of feel that way too—like, it gets easier to adjust after you've done it before."

"Yeah, but my transition was nothing like yours—at least with mine it was the same country, same language, same family, and everything."

She nodded. "True, but do not discount your adjustment either. It's hard anytime you move to a new place." She unconsciously reached up to touch the heart-shaped necklace that hung about her neck as memories of her childhood home began to fill her mind's eye.

"Did you move around a lot after we stopped talking?" Chase asked.

She nodded. "Yes, my family moved but then I went off to college. After college, though, I went off the grid to get away from him and moved all over."

"I see. I guess that made it hard to have someone special in your life?"

She turned and saw his beautiful blue eyes watching her face in the fading sunlight; there was a sense of vulnerability in his expression, a genuine desire to know.

Slowly, she nodded. "Yeah, it did. But—" she stopped.

"But what?" he asked, his voice soft.

She gazed off into the distance as the sun reached the horizon, casting shadows all over. "But..." again she paused and he waited. For a moment she watched as a squirrel jumped in the grass then fled into the trees. Turning back to Chase, she brought her deep brown eyes up to meet his from across the table, "but I had already met someone special and," she paused, "and I'd lost him."

Slowly, he stood up and walked over to her side of the table. Putting his hand out, he waited for her to put her hand into his before he gently helped her up. Slowly pulling her close, he wrapped his muscular arms around her small frame in a warm embrace. "I did too, but it looks like I've found her again."

For a moment, time stood still and Sarah felt herself covered in feelings of warmth, love, and protection. This man had been there for her when they were younger—he had read her every letter, every *rambling* letter. He had responded to every single one with intensity and interest. He had never acted bored or called anything petty but instead had listened and responded with enthusiasm and interest. And through those letters, they had become close friends, and in many ways, lovers. Now—despite life ripping them apart—he stood here with her, wanting her. The feeling was almost overwhelming.

She pulled back and looked at his bright blue eyes in the faded sunlight. "But what if we're different now? What if I'm not the girl you remember?"

"Then I want to learn about who you are now, Sarah," Chase said gently as he slowly pushed back a strain of hair that was covering her face. "I've waited for you, Sarah. When we met, I knew there was something very special about you and then we got so close. When we lost contact and I couldn't find you despite my best efforts, there was a gap inside me. And now that I've found you again, I want to know the person you are now." He paused. "That is, if you'll let me."

Putting her head against his chest, she replied, her voice soft, "Absolutely."

CHAPTER SIX

The sun rose from the horizon casting a beautiful array of purple and orange. A woman sat outside on her run-down, screened-in porch looking towards the sunrise, but her mind did not comprehend its beauty. She sat there, motionless; her psyche so damaged she could no longer feel the happy feeling that a person experiences when witnessing such beauty. She could not feel the peace that comes when most of nature is asleep or the excitement when the entire world is slowly waking up.

Instead, she sat there motionless and stared straight ahead with a cup of tea in her hand. She had not drunk a sip of the tea nor eaten anything in days. Her body was thin and frail and she was barely holding on to life— but what was life? Her life was miserable, lonely, and painful. If it were not for the slight hope of one day finding the daughter who had run away, she would not be alive. In fact, many days she considered waiting until Richard left for work and then doing the deed herself. She knew that there were things worse than death, and living this way was worse.

Other days, she reasoned that if Richard got angry enough, he would kill her himself. And yet, the smallest bit of her old, stubborn self would reappear and convince her not to let him do that, for then he would be the winner.

"Sarah," the woman muttered softly, "my girl, where are you? Are you safe? Will I ever see you again?"

"Ma'am!" a loud voice said from the neighbor's yard. "Ma'am!" The older man walked quickly towards her porch. "Ma'am, your dog is digging up my garden. If you don't do something about it, I am going to call the dog catcher and get him taken care of, this is ridiculous! Do you know how much trouble and money I have put into this garden?"

The man walked up onto the porch and through the screened door. "I don't have a dog," The woman responded.

"Don't care. If you don't do anything to get that rascal out of my yard, I'll call this here dog catcher myself!" The man handed her a business card. "Call this number yourself and get this dog gone!" The older man winked at her and then turned and walked off the porch.

She turned and read the card. On the front it said: "Michael James, Dogcatcher. Asheville, NC." Flipping the card over, she saw a number written along with the words, "Call him before it's too late." Surprised, she looked up to see the man gone.

LOCATION: CHAITI
TIME: PRESENT DAY

The darkness within the cave was deep and the torch did little to lighten the cave as Ajahadé looked at the large punching bags hanging from the ceiling and other equipment–including dummies–within the cave. *The key to fighting is to identify your enemy's weakness and exploit it as soon as possible in order to incapacitate him as quickly as possible.* With solid skill and precision, she began fighting violently. Slamming her fists into the bag time and time again, she rejected any feelings of pain and kept going. *Pain is just your body signaling that the fight is getting shorter. You must ignore the pain and keep fighting until you win.*

But another kind of pain began to creep in...images of her family appeared before her eyes: her young son with his wild and imaginative eyes overflowing with excitement for life; her loving husband with his strong arms that had been strengthened by the hard labor he had done to keep his family financially sound; and their two little girls with their brown eyes and curly hair. The aching, the longing within Ajahadé was intense–she yearned for them and yet knew the hard truth: she would never see them again.

She kicked her leg into the bag with anger and strength. "I can't have those scumbags win," she said out loud and kicked again, this time even stronger.

Ajahadé recalled Jarah's expression as she had learned of her baby's death and seen his lifeless little body. She heard the heart-wrenching screams and tears of agony as reality set in as Jarah realized that everyone she loved was gone. All of them had been taken by the hands of the cruel and ruthless enemy.

Ajahadé slammed her left fist even harder. She kicked with all her strength. *They cannot get away with this. They are evil, ruthless scumbags with no sense of humanity. They kill with no regard for human life.*

But then, as if on cue, fear began to creep in... *Because of you, many people died. You missed it–the evidence was all there and yet you failed to see it. You could have prevented it and you didn't. The only reason you are still alive now is because you've kept your head down and the Mashottiís do not know you are alive. One move and they will know and they will seek you out and everyone close to you will be tortured and killed– including Ish and his family.*

Images of Ishnomela and his sweet, loving family appeared before her mind: his kind, eldest son who had rushed to her aid and helped her carry Jarah; his middle child who was always quiet but held the same sense of intelligence that his father possessed; and the youngest child who was always into something– whether that was throwing a rock or knocking over his father's woodpile by accident. Then there was Ishnomela's lovely wife who was constantly working to provide for the needs of her family and–though she didn't understand Ishnomela's mysterious side–she was always supportive of his pursuits. *I can't let anything happen to them. I have to continue to keep my head down and not let the Mashottiís know that I'm alive.*

Frustrated by the situation, she fought harder...and harder....until her strength was depleted.

LOCATION: UNITED STATES OF AMERICA
TIME: SEVERAL DAYS LATER

"So, tell me about your work," Chase said as they walked very slowly (his right leg was now out of the cast and into a medical boot) through the flower garden, Zeus trotting along beside them.

"Well, not much to it, really. I work at the retirement home where your grandmother stayed while she was recovering from her surgery."

He nodded in memory. "What do you do there?"

"I coordinate activities for them. Since they are stranded there, I try to make their lives more exciting and active, so I coordinate music concerts, games, hair appointments, outings, etc."

"What kind of concerts?" he asked as they rounded the corner and reached the fountain. They both sat down on the nearby bench.

"Mostly bluegrass bands since those are the only ones that'll come for little-to-no cost. Our budget is quite small, so many of them are just volunteers."

Chase put his arm around her and pulled her closer. "I see. That makes sense. About how many people usually show up for the concerts?"

Sarah thought for a minute. "It depends on the band, but most of the time less than 50 people come out."

He nodded. "Well, I'm not bluegrass, but if you ever

want me to come sing, I'm happy to come."

Sarah's face lit up. "You would?"

"Yes," he smiled, "but on one condition."

"Oh?"

"Yeah," he said, a teasing smile dancing around his lips.

"And what would that condition be?"

"That a beautiful woman—aka, you—play the piano for me." She smiled and felt her face getting warm.

"I haven't played in years, Chase."

"Why not?"

She thought for a long moment before responding, "I think I just kinda lost my desire. I mean, music is my expression—it's an expression of my inner self, a way of communicating that words cannot fulfill—and it just hurt too much at certain times."

He nodded in understanding. "I get that."

"But—" she paused, "I would love to hear you sing again. The cassette tapes you sent me have long worn out."

He giggled. "Are you serious? You kept those things?"

She smiled. "Of course! How could I have gotten rid of

them? I loved them!"

He pulled her closer and hugged her tightly. "You're awesome, Sarah. I really missed you."

Looking up into his beautiful blue eyes, she spoke, her voice soft, "I missed you too, Chase."

LOCATION: CHAITI
TIME: SEVERAL DAYS LATER

It was dark, but Ajahadé saw armed men approaching. They were slowly creeping down the familiar hill toward a hut: her brother's hut. With skill, they surrounded the hut and suddenly brought fire. The darkness exploded in sharp bursts of light and gunshots until suddenly one of the men threw a grenade into the middle of the hut. The whole group of men scattered to the woods just as the entire hut exploded.

No! Ajahadé yelled.

Then suddenly, it all vanished.

Sitting up, she realized it had all been a dream. But something was still not right. The animals and creatures outside the hut were not making their normal, peaceful sounds and in her heart was a feeling that she could not shake. *Something is wrong with Ish.*

Slowly standing up, she changed clothes, secured her knife around her leg and her gun behind her back. With nearly-silent footsteps, she walked outside and into the night.

After several long minutes of walking in the woods, she approached the familiar hill. Pausing, she looked down at Ishnomela's hut below and knew her fears were right: his hut was ruined.

Just like Jarah's house, everything around it was disarrayed and the roof was gone. Her body tensed. With her gun in position, she quietly crept down the hill towards the hut. Once she reached it, she put her back against the clay wall and stood still to listen. For several long moments, she stayed there, ready to fire at anything that approached. But there was only eerie silence.

She crept closer to the door and paused outside the doorway to listen. With skills cultivated through years of experience, she lunged into the hut, gun in position and ready to fight the Mashotiis inside.

There was no one there to fight her. *They're gone,* she thought as she looked around the hut. Everything within it was destroyed. The pots and pans were thrown onto the floor; the blankets they used as beds were ripped into shreds. The only photograph they owned was ripped out of its frame and torn into pieces on the dirt floor. *Typical Mashottii style—spare nothing, destroy it all.*

But still something was slightly off. For a moment, she stood there trying to figure out what it was but she could not. *Something is not quite the way they always do it...but what?* Knowing that the longer she stood there, the higher her risk of being captured would be, she took one final mental picture of the hut and exited.

Once in the safety of the woods, the gravity of the situation hit her. *I cannot go home. On the slight chance that they know I'm alive, I will be their next target.* She disappeared into the dark woods.

A little while later, she approached a mountain with rocky ledges. Pushing several large, heavy rocks away from the opening, she crawled into a small cave and disappeared into the mountain. The cave was small, barely large enough for her to crawl through it. The smell of dirt filled her nose, as she dragged her knees and hands across the dirt floor. She could hear dripping from an underground stream deep inside the cave. In the absence of light, she used that noise and a small indentation on the rock wall to guide her towards her destination. The deeper she went, the larger the cave became until finally it was large enough for her to stand.

She felt a slight pain in her knees as she stood up but ignored it. She trudged further into the cave and took a sharp right and then a left until she reached the underground room. It was dark and cold but, despite this, it held a sense of hope—hope of escape.

Feeling alongside the wall, she walked to the far end of the room and felt a door. She moved her hand down the doorframe until she reached the floor. Dragging her hand to the left, she felt a device sitting on the floor beside the door. Using it, she initiated the secret signal.

Keeping her hand on wall to guide her, she walked to the right until she felt a large crack next to a protruding rock. Reaching into the crack, she pulled out a small package and concealed it within her shirt. Walking back to the other side of the room, she sat down behind the door and waited in the silence, except for the dripping of the creek nearby.

After several long moments had passed, she heard footsteps approaching from the other side of the door. The door unlatched and opened. An older man with a full gray beard appeared with a torch in his weathered hand. Instantly, Ajahadé recognized him and stood up. "Hi, Bahja," she said in Chaitian.

"Ajahadé, ma'am," he slightly bowed in her presence. "I thought it was you."

"Yes, indeed."

"How may I help you, ma'am?" he asked in their language.

"For reasons I cannot explain, I need to get off the island. Could you arrange that for me?"

"When?"

"Tonight."

"Yes ma'am." His deep voice was full of respect. "Wait here and I will get you out." He then disappeared behind the door.

He was gone for what seemed like hours—but was probably only a few minutes—and then returned. "Ma'am?"

"Yes," Ajahadé responded, her voice emotionless.

"I've got you a helicopter that can take you to the next island. There you will find a private plane waiting for you and it will take you to Hawaii. Once you are in Hawaii, you can go wherever you need to go. Just tell the pilot of the private plane where you want to go, and he will arrange your flight."

Ajahadé nodded. "Thank you, Bahja."

"You're welcome, ma'am. I'm glad I can help you."

Ajahadé turned towards him and brought her gaze up to make direct eye contact. When she spoke, her voice was very serious. "Seriously, thank you. I would be wrong if I didn't tell you but–" she paused, "it is dangerous. Please come with me."

The older man's eyes spread in surprise. "Ma'am," he paused, "I respect you highly but I must decline. This was our plan and I agreed to do this many years ago. I do it knowing the risks and accepting them for the sake of my country. If I die, I die because I helped my people–our people–and that is worth the risk for me."

Ajahadé looked up at him. "I respect your decision and thank you." She paused. "It is very dangerous, Bahja, so please promise me that you'll at least be careful."

The older man nodded and then led her up the stairs.

CHAPTER SEVEN

Its slick, black figure enticed Sarah into the room while its white keys beckoned for her to touch them. Though years had passed by with no contact with piano keys, she could not resist their call. Dr. Mychael was at a church function and Chase was on a business phone call, so she reasoned, *no one will hear me playing.*

She walked slowly into Dr. Mychael's music room and up to the piano. For a moment, she looked at the beautiful instrument: it was by far the nicest one she had ever come near. She wasn't sure how much it cost exactly but from the make, quality, and brand she knew it cost more than the average car and probably as much as a small house in the south.

Pulling out the bench covered in leather, she sat down. Taking a deep breath, she touched one of the keys. The sound was impeccable and the keys were quick to respond to her touch. The instrument begged for more;

it wanted to be touched, to be played. So, with soft and gentle movements, she began playing a familiar song. The partnership between Sarah and the piano began to pull at each emotion bubbling up from below the surface and enticed the emotions upward to express themselves in ways words could not allow. With each key her small hands touched, the emotional expression grew in intensity as all the built-up feelings—all the things she could not say in words—came flooding out. They grew so intense that her memorized songs were no longer enough to express the emotions and she began improvising as each note drew her into the next.

After a while of improvisation, she transitioned to a familiar song—a song that had helped her to survive in many situations by calming her fears—and began playing CJ's song "You Are Gone." The song had been there for her during the hard times she had faced while on the run. Its beautiful melody had helped her when she had been followed and needed to move again by calming the fear that had gripped her and made her frozen, unable to move. That song—and the sound of the beautiful masculine voice that sang it—had calmed and soothed her in her darkest of nights. And today, she played it nearly flawlessly on the epitome of pianos.

As the beautiful melody of CJ's song flew through the air, it was gradually joined by another sound that was off in the distance but growing stronger. Sarah listened but did not believe her ears: it was a voice quite similar to the voice that had sung the song so many times before through her music player. The beautiful, strong voice—with depth and precision—communicated feelings of loss, love and care so profoundly it seemed as though it was coming from the depths of the singer's heart.

The sound grew stronger and she looked up to see Chase approaching the doorway. He stopped and stood there singing with her. His incredible voice met the notes of the piano and merged to form a breathtaking sound—but it was more than just a sound. It was a communication of two individuals who cared so much for one another that words could not portray their feelings and yet music—in its beauty and genius—could. All the feelings of love, loss, and pain of the past joined with happiness of the present.

Overwhelmed with the feelings she was both expressing and receiving, Sarah poured her heart into the music just as her mind began to wonder: *Is Chase the same person as CJ?* But just as fast as that thought appeared, so did her memory of what CJ—the pop star—was like as he conducted his shows. He did them with such showmanship and flamboyancy that it did not match the humble person she knew as Chase. *No, it cannot be the same person. Chase is far too humble and down-to-earth to be someone like that...*

Chase took a few steps further into the room, approached her side, and then sat down on the bench beside her. Their song grew softer before growing in intensity as she pushed aside all wandering thoughts and focused solely on communicating her feelings with the man she loved.

Gradually softening the notes as the song neared the end, Sarah played the final chord. Looking up at Chase, their eyes locked and her heart jumped. She felt a connection so strong—so beautiful—that words could not express it. He leaned towards her and she leaned closer. Their faces near one another, she looked into his bright blue eyes and saw a man who cared for her deeply—who wanted her. She saw a man she wanted and—despite the years away from each other—still cared for him deeply. She felt connected to him like she had to no other person in her life.

She leaned even closer and he shifted to put his arm around her when suddenly fear reared its ugly head. Suddenly, she didn't see the kind, gentle Chase but instead she saw mean and vicious Richard. Her whole body tensed and her hands began to tremble. Taking a deep breath, she tried to calm her nerves but her body was already panicking—it was prepared for the hurt and pain of Richard's sexual advances.

Chase pulled back and looked at her. "Are you okay?" She shook her head but could not speak—fear was gripping her throat. "What's wrong? Please, tell me." His bright blue eyes were searching her face with such worry and concern it made her heart ache.

"I—I'm scared," she stuttered, barely able to speak.

He paused as his loving eyes showed he was thinking hard. "What did I do to scare you?"

"Nothing," she said immediately. "It—it's a ghost from the past."

"Like a flashback?" His voice was soft.

She nodded, "I—I want to kiss you so badly, but—" she paused, "but being looked at like that and being touched triggered something."

He looked thoughtful for a moment as he processed what she had just said. Then he replied, his voice soft and each word carefully chosen, "Sarah, you have no idea how much it burns me up that he treated you like that; it makes me so mad that someone would do something like that to someone I care about so much. It's awful." He paused and she turned her face up to meet his eyes. "But Sarah, I'm not him and I would *never* hurt you. I love you—I don't want to see you get hurt."

Sarah felt a lump grow in her throat as his words landed in her heart. *He loves me,* she thought and felt his loving words fighting the fear within. She felt the fear beginning to retreat. For a moment, she stayed silent as she processed what had just been said.

"I know you wouldn't hurt me, but the fear is still there sometimes."

He nodded in understanding. "Grandmother has told me about how that happens."

Sarah nodded. "In me?"

"In general," he responded. "She compared it to soldiers who relate loud noises to gunshots and feeling like they have to respond to them appropriately in order to survive. When they get back to the US and hear a car back-fire, they *know* it isn't a gunshot but the fear is still there."

"And their bodies respond as though it's a gunshot,"

she added, her voice quiet.

He nodded. "And she said it's similar with people who've been abused. They see signs that they saw before, and their bodies go into a 'get ready for hurt' mode automatically."

"Exactly," Sarah responded. "And mine has been programmed to think that looks and touches like that are signs that I'm about to be violated."

"Not with me, Sarah. I won't kiss or even hug you if you don't want it. You're in control." For some reason, those words were exactly what she needed. They calmed her fear and replaced it with feelings of warmth, love, and safety.

She leaned into his chest and pulled his muscular arms around her shoulders. Quietly, she spoke, "Thank you, Chase." She paused. "I love you."

Hugging her tighter, he smiled and responded, "I love you too, Sarah."

LOCATION: SOUTH CAROLINA

Her boney, wrinkled hands trembled in fear as she slowly picked up the cordless phone. She looked at the business card with the dogcatcher's name and number one more time and took a deep breath. Slowly, she dialed the number.

"Hello," a man's voice said on the other end.

"Y—yes," the older woman stuttered, "is this Michael James, the dogcatcher?"

There was a pause on the other side of the phone. "No, but I'll get him for you. One second." A few moments later, a man answered the phone.

"Is this Mrs. Daniels?"

"Yes," the older lady responded. "I was told to contact you."

"Yes, I wanted to tell you I saw someone who may fit the description of your daughter walking a dog in this area."

Instantly, the woman's heart skipped a beat. "You did? Where? What did she look like? Was she okay?"

"Ma'am," the man said from the other side of the phone, "calm down. It is only speculation at this point. It's not been confirmed, but I wanted to let you know that we may have found something. Call me again in a week's time, and I'll give you more details."

"A week?" Mrs. Daniels responded, bewildered by the vagueness of his answer. But before the man could respond, Mrs. Daniels heard a noise coming from the driveway. Without another word, she hung up the phone and put it back on the charger. A few seconds later, Richard walked inside, his eyes glaring at his wife.

"You've done something," he said, his voice low and suspicious. Mrs. Daniels shook her head and watched as the large man slowly walked towards the phone that hung on the wall. Picking it up, he dialed a three-digit number that would give him the number that was last called from that phone. She watched as he wrote down the number that the automated system gave him.

Her body began to tremble as he turned and looked at her, his beady eyes wild and full of angry intent. "Asheville, NC! Why would you call there? Do you have a lover?"

He stormed over to her and balled his hand into a fist. "Tell me woman! Who is he!"

"No one," Mrs. Daniels responded, her chin quivering in fear. "You are the only man in my life."

"Pssh!" Richard said angrily and drew his hand up. Without a moment of hesitation, he slammed his fist against her face with such force that she fell out of the chair and onto the floor.

She wrenched in pain and curled her frail body into a circle. "Woman! Tell me!" he yelled again and kicked her in the back. She felt pain shoot through her kidneys. He kicked her again.

He paused for a moment and stared at her. "You really are not going to tell me what that call was about?" he asked. "If it's about our daughter, you know I have the right to know just as much as you do. She is *my* daughter." Mrs. Daniels stayed silent. It only angered him more. He kicked her again.

"Tell me!" he yelled to his badly bruised and beaten wife. "Was it about Sarah?"

Weakened, Mrs. Daniels slowly looked up at him. Her eyes were so swollen she could barely see, but she made out the blurry shape of him standing above her, a metal baseball bat in his hand. Slowly, she nodded and everything went completely black.

LOCATION: ABOVE PACIFIC ISLANDS

The jet jerked and woke Ajahadé. Slowly opening her eyes, she looked out the window to see the islands coming into sight below. The mountainous range was lush with vegetation—clearly not experiencing a drought like Chaiti—and surrounded by crystal clear water.

Hearing someone approaching, she looked up to see the only flight attendant on the private jet walking up. "Ma'am," she said keeping her gaze down and not meeting Ajahade's eyes as was customary to show respect to a high-ranking person, "the pilot told me to tell you to prepare for landing." She reached into her pocket and pulled out a small envelope. "And he said to give you this."

"Thank you," Ajahadé responded and took the envelope. On the outside of the sealed envelope was a familiar symbol. Ajahadé waited until the flight attendant had disappeared into the cockpit before opening the letter. Inside was a single set of numbers. Without blinking an eye, Ajahadé knew exactly what they meant.

Pulling out the bag that she had taken from the cave, she checked its contents. *All my papers are here along with enough cash to get me through; good.*

Now knowing that her resources were available, she continued devising her plan.

LOCATION: UNITED STATES OF AMERICA
TIME: SEVERAL DAYS LATER

The sun shone brightly in the cloudless sky as Sarah and Chase slowly walked along the wooden trail, Zeus trotting along ahead. "How are you feeling?" Sarah asked, looking down at Chase's still-recovering legs.

"Okay so far. We may have to stop in a little while though."

"Okay, just let me know," Sarah said as she looked down at her own feet, which were screaming with claustrophobia. Stopping, she removed her sneakers.

Chase stopped and looked at her. "Going barefoot?"

"Yeah," she responded and took off her socks. Placing her shoes at the base of the tree near the path, she started walking again.

"Have you always done that?" Chase asked.

"Yeah," Sarah said again, "I just feel restrained if I wear shoes too long, especially when I'm walking in the woods."

"You aren't afraid of sticks or rocks hurting them?"

"Naw," Sarah waved her hand, "I've been walking in woods barefoot since I *could* walk, so my feet are tough."

"Your parents let you go barefoot growing up?" He looked surprised.

"My first family, yes, because shoes were a luxury, and when we had them, we only used them on special occasions."

Chase nodded in understanding. "Oh, that makes sense." Sarah nodded and watched as two birds landed in a tree. They fought and screeched at each other before flying off into the distance.

"So, speaking of childhoods, tell me a childhood story," Sarah said, looking over at Chase who had slowed his pace even more.

"Okay," he said and thought for a long moment. "Well, back when my family lived in Georgia, we had a friend who had horses." He paused, stopping next to a tree to take a break. Leaning against the tree, he continued, "So, my brother and I decided to go horseback riding. I hadn't ridden before, so I was a bit scared, but I definitely was not going to tell anyone that."

"Oh yeah. Can't let people know you're scared," Sarah said teasingly with a smile dancing on her face.

"Of course not," Chase smiled. "So, instead of letting them know I had no idea how to tell the horse to go, stop, turn, etc., I decided that I was smart enough to figure it out. I would just watch my brother and see what he did."

"Seems logical."

"It was, except he had no idea what he was doing either and didn't want to admit it either."

Sarah laughed.

"Anyway, we got the horses, tied them up next to the barn and went inside the barn to get the saddles."

"Okay, and—" Sarah let the sentence hang.

"And we saw three saddles all slightly different shapes but approximately the same size, so we had no idea which one went for each horse." He paused. "So I—very confidently—grabbed one that looked nice and then took it back outside."

He sat down under the tree. Sarah followed. "And I approached the horse with the saddle. The horse kinda gave me this sideways look like 'Hey man, what are ya doing?' and in my head I thought, *I have no idea how to put on a saddle but it can't be that hard. I've seen people do it in movies.* So I pulled the saddle up in my hands and threw it over the horse," he giggled. "The only problem was, I threw it too hard, and it went flying over the top of the horse."

Sarah laughed, revealing her white teeth.

"So I—somewhat less confidently now—walked over to the other side of the horse and picked up the saddle. I saw out the corner of my eye the horse giving me another look, but again I ignored it. This time I threw the saddle across his back. And I was like, 'Yes! I have this.'"

"Nice but did you put a—"

"Wait for it," Chase said, a smile teasing his lips again.

"I know what you're thinking." She smiled and then waited for him to continue. "So I went up to the saddle that was now on his back and I looked at the straps. They didn't look too hard—just like an oversized belt—so I buckled up the saddle on him. And I thought I was good."

"Okay—"

"Well, then it occurred to me that I've never actually mounted a horse, so I wasn't really sure how to get on." He paused. "But there were the stirrups, so I figured I'd put my foot in there like a step."

She smiled so hard she was almost laughing. "It isn't a step."

"Exactly, it isn't built like that but I was young and dumb so I stood on the right side of the horse and put my left foot in the stirrup. Then, like an idiot, I paused trying to figure out what to do with my right foot because I couldn't exactly flop it over the horse, and my left foot was now stuck in the stirrup."

Sarah laughed. "You were supposed to put your left foot in the stirrup and swing your right over the saddle."

"Well, that would have made perfect sense but I wasn't even thinking. At this point, I just wanted to act like I knew what I was doing and get off onto the trail before my brother got his horse ready."

"So, what happened?"

"Well, my foot was stuck in the stirrup. I lost my balance

and fell backwards. So I was literally hanging off the side of the horse."

Sarah laughed hard. "Oh man, and what was the horse doing?"

"It kind of just stood there like, 'O-M-G, what an idiot.'" Sarah laughed harder and Chase laughed, revealing his straight, white teeth.

"Anyway, so finally I managed to power my weight upwards enough to grab the saddle and pull myself up on top of the horse." He paused. "But then the horse let out a big breath and the entire saddle slid to one side. I slid off the horse and landed on the ground with one big thud."

Sarah laughed so hard she could barely breathe. "Were you okay?"

Chase nodded, still laughing. "Yeah, I was fine but by this time the owner of the horse had come up. Unbeknownst to me at the time, she had seen basically the whole thing."

"Oh man, what did she do?"

"She laughed at me and then explained everything I'd done wrong—including getting the wrong saddle and even forgetting to put a saddle blanket on the horse."

Sarah laughed. "That is hilarious. Did you end up being able to ride?"

"Yeah, eventually, after getting a nice, long lesson on

horseback riding."

Sarah smiled. "Well, at least you got to ride."

"True," Chase responded. "And it was quite fun."

"Isn't it?" Sarah's face lit up in excitement. "It's just a great feeling—like you are so free."

"Yes! It is an amazing feeling. I wouldn't want the upkeep of a horse, but riding is definitely very fun. Where did you ride?"

"Back home," Sarah responded and became somewhat distant as memories of her native land came up in her mind. "My mum and I used to ride the horses at her work. They were really nice horses, and we'd ride them along trails since they were quiet and could go over much rougher terrain than cars could. Plus, we didn't have a car anyway."

"That makes sense," Chase responded. "It seems like such a different way of life."

"Yes, it really was. It was like a step back in time."

"I'm sure. I can imagine adjusting to the US was difficult."

"It was, especially with all the sensory information. It was—and still is sometimes—overwhelming."

"What do you mean?"

"Well, all the unnatural sounds. You know, like car

engines, music, machinery, etc. It's a lot of sounds and things to process at once."

Chase nodded. "Is that why you like the woods so much?"

"Yeah, that's exactly why. It reminds me of home a little bit." She paused. "The piano does as well."

"How so?"

"There used to be a piano at my mum's work and one of the people there taught me how to play."

Chase nodded. "That's really neat."

Sarah nodded and then looked at Chase. "Ready to keep going?"

CHAPTER EIGHT

The sun had just dipped below the horizon and the moon started ascending into the sky when Ajahadé began changing her clothes and preparing for the night ahead from inside the single-story motel. She put on a black shirt, pants, and shoes, and looked into the mirror. *This should be dark enough not to stand out and to allow me to escape into the woods, if needed.*

Brushing her dark black hair, she pulled it back into a half-ponytail and grabbed her bag. Outside, a taxi waited for her. Entering, she told the cab driver an address and sat back to think. This was a day she had thought may come but never really believed it would: the day her beloved brother and family vanished without a trace. Now, it was up to her to find them and ensure their safety before the Mashottiís killed them all—and that was assuming they were still alive.

The trick was that—because the Mashottiís had gotten Ishnomela—they probably knew she was alive now. This greatly limited her ability to find her family, but she was not giving up. There was a way—it was just a matter of finding it.

The cab driver slowed the car and pulled up to the shopping center. Giving him money and thanking him, Ajahadé exited the vehicle and slowly walked towards the shopping center. Just when the cab driver was out of sight, she turned and walked behind the shopping center and into the woods.

Under the cover of night and the dense forest, she began jogging through the woods, relying only on the route she had plotted out earlier that day and her natural instincts to keep her on track. After several long minutes, she heard the sound of cars on the road ahead. *This must be right,* she thought and followed the sound. The woods stopped at the road, and so did she.

Turning left, she walked between the edge of the road and the woods until she spotted her target: a large, cement fence with an iron gate and guard house. Getting close, she saw a guard standing outside the gate, a huge gun in front of him.

She cleared her throat so as not to alarm him and waited until he looked up to see her approaching. She took a few more steps forward and then stopped in front of him. "Good evening, sir," she said in Chaitian. She watched his tense shoulders relax a little bit at the sound of his native language.

"Good evening, ma'am," he responded in Chaitian. "Credentials?"

She nodded and then stuck out her hand. "This is all I have left." She pointed to her fingertips.

The guard nodded and then stepped into the guardhouse and brought out a device. Putting her right hand on the device, she watched as it scanned her fingers and then flashed a screen that stated "Unable to Process."

"It's probably the scars," she said. "Could we do the other hand?"

The guard nodded and helped her put her left hand onto the device. Within a few minutes, the screen changed to approval. The guard nodded and hit a lever that enabled the huge iron gate to open up.

Walking inside, she passed another series of armed guards before finally entering the building and sitting down in the foyer. After a few moments, a familiar bodyguard with thick black hair and dark eyes walked into the foyer.

"Aj!" he exclaimed with excitement. "Ma'am, I never thought I would see you here. It's good to see you alive."

Ajahadé smiled at the pessimism and stood up to greet him. "Thank you, Jahdej, it's good to see you, too."

"Here to see the Chief?" he asked knowingly.

"Yes," Ajahadé responded, "Would that be possible?"

Jahdej looked serious. "For anyone else, absolutely

not. But for you, he'd kill me if I turned you away."

"Well," Ajahadé responded with an equally serious tone, "we certainly would not want that."

"No, we wouldn't," he responded and then asked her to follow him down a long hallway. After a little while, he led her into a large room with dim lighting and a large oak desk in the center. *Chief Sengj's office,* she thought as she took a seat in the corner.

"He'll be with you in a moment," Jahdej responded. Ajahadé nodded her thanks and he left. After several long minutes, the former leader of Chaiti, Chief Sengj, appeared. She instantly bowed in his presence.

"Please, rise," the familiar voice said, in Chaitian, and she stood. "Look," he said, asking her to break customs and look at him in the eye. Obeying his request, Ajahadé looked up to his gray eyes. She instantly remembered how she used to steal glances at those eyes when she was a young soldier under his command. They always told her more than his words. Today was no different; his eyes held a look she had not seen before. It was a look of deep relief; almost as though he was a father suddenly realizing the daughter he thought had been dead was alive.

"Aj," he said, his voice low, as he pushed back his thick gray hair. "Indeed you *are* alive."

A small smile teased her lips. "Yes, I am," she said, respectfully.

"I know how you are so I thought you would survive, but

then I got no word from or about you for so many years that I was losing hope."

"I went dark," she said, her voice lacking emotion. "It was the best thing to do."

His face searched hers as though trying to read what she was saying beyond her words. After several moments, he turned and walked towards the window. Looking outside, he spoke, "And what brings you into the sunlight?"

"Ish has vanished," she said, her voice still emotionless.

Without showing any emotion, he spoke, "Do you think he was taken or vanished on his own?"

"His house was ruined—roof removed, belongings destroyed, and door knocked down. Neither he nor his family was anywhere in sight."

"Any blood on the floor?"

"Yes, but only drippings—not puddles."

Chief Sengj looked deep in thought. "And what do you think happened?"

"I'm unsure. At first glance it appeared to be done by the Mashottiís but—" she paused, "but something is off—" She let the sentence hang.

He turned to look at her. "Gut feeling?"

"Sort of," she responded, "but I keep walking back through the house in my head trying to figure out what prompted the feeling. There had to be something tangible that triggered it."

Chief Sengj nodded. "Yes, indeed." He turned and sat down at a chair near hers. "Walk me through what you found, and let's see if we can spot it."

So she did. Piece by piece, she described how she found Ishonomela's hut. When she got to the point of describing the picture, she stopped. "That's it—the picture."

Chief Sengj nodded. "Yep, the Mashottiís would not have ripped it and put the pieces on the floor. They would have burned it as a symbol of their victory."

"Agreed." Ajahadé looked out the window in thought. "So, who could have gotten them?"

"Maybe no one," Chief Sengj responded matter-of-factly.

Ajahadé turned to look at him. "Are you implying that Ish may have faked his own kidnapping?"

Chief Sengj nodded. "He could have. That way the Mashottiís would think that he was already captured or killed and would not search for him and his family."

Ajahadé thought hard. "But that would be assuming they are so disorganized that they have not communicated to the top ranks what they had done." Chief Sengj nodded. "But—" Ajahadé paused. "Faking a disappearance would also force me to try to find him thereby getting me involved in the war..." Her voice trailed off.

"Perhaps," Chief Sengj responded, "but it is not unreasonable to think that Mashottiís are not good at communicating and could see his kidnapping as a victory."

Ajahadé looked at him, her eyes trying to decipher what he was implying. She thought for a moment before responding. "Ish said they are strong in might but—at least in the beginning—we were outsmarting them with our strategies. Are you implying they are disorganized and uncommunicative as well?"

Without hesitation, the diplomat responded, "Absolutely." He stood up and walked over to his desk. He pulled out a large poster-sized piece of paper and spread it across his large oak desk. He motioned for Ajahadé to come over.

On the paper was a map of Chaiti along with red and blue X marks placed on certain villages. "These here," he pointed to the red X marks, "are places that the Mashottiís have destroyed while the blue ones are places we still have." He paused to let Ajahadé take in the information.

"Interesting," she said and let the sentence hang for a moment while she looked at each city. "So, the ones they have taken are the small ones or the ones that have mostly civilians without military backgrounds."

"Exactly," he responded matter-of-factly. "They've taken

the easy targets." He paused. "But the hard targets where most of our former military folks live and those who worked in my regime," he pointed to several villages on the map, "those, they have not yet touched."

Ajahadé thought hard. "So, it appears like they are making more progress than they actually are."

"And they are making a lot of progress, don't get me wrong. Look at all the cities they have already taken but," he paused, "they aren't making as much progress as it appears."

Ajahadé stared at the map for several more minutes before speaking, "But they are running out of easy targets."

Chief Sengj nodded. "So they are going to need a strategy soon and a good one at that. Right now we are protecting the hard targets well by sheer strategy, but if they get wind of our strategy or come up with a good strategy of their own, we are toast."

"So this is a critical point in the war," Ajahadé responded, her tone serious.

"Yes, right now—or soon—is essentially the point within the war that will most likely determine the outcome." He paused and asked her to look at him. When she complied, he spoke, "Aj, this is where you come in. I need you to—" she instantly started shaking her head and he stopped.

"I can't get too involved. I just came here to see if you knew anything about Ish that could help me find him.

Once I find him, I'm going back into the dark."

Chief Sengj's wrinkled face flashed disappointment before returning to his default emotionless expression. For several moments, he stayed silent as though taken back by her words. He walked back over to the window and looked out. The moments stretched on.

Finally, he turned to look at her. "Ish told me you wouldn't help but didn't explain why. Could you please enlighten me?"

Ajahadé paused at such a direct question coming from the man she respected more than anyone else—the man who with just one word could have her killed instantly— and who she had dedicated her life to protect and serve as a soldier and, later, his advisor. Biting her lower lip, she then cleared her throat and began, "After what happened, I cannot forgive myself. My family, Chief—" she paused. "They all died because of me. Even precious Chrystalia—your only granddaughter—died because of me."

Chief Sengj walked over and sat down next to her. He waited for her eyes to reach his before he spoke, "No," he said firmly. "Ajahadé, those people did not die because of you. There was nothing you could have done to prevent that."

"But there was—" She let the sentence hang.

"There was what?"

"I had pieces of information and I should have put them together and figured out their plan."

Chief Sengj looked serious. "Aj, you told me all that you knew at that time, correct?"

"Yes sir," she nodded.

"And even I did not put the pieces together. And frankly, recalling the pieces in my head now I can see their evil plan, but that's only because I use the additional knowledge that I have now–hindsight. There was no way we could have put it together and known what they were going to do."

Ajahadé still looked doubtful. "Okay," he responded, "if you don't believe that, at least share the guilt." A confused look crossed her face and he continued, "You gave me the pieces as well and / did not put them together either. On the chance that it could have been put together, then I am in just as much at fault as you are."

"No, you aren't," she responded. "It was my responsibility as your advisor and I failed. Your regime was toppled, and everyone except you and me died because of that."

His face grew very serious. "No, my regime was overtaken for numerous reasons, mainly because I trusted in people I should not have. People betrayed me–even my own daughter–and I should not have trusted them." He stood up and walked over to the shelf behind his desk. On the shelf sat a safe. Punching a code into the safe, he opened it and pulled out an envelope. He walked back over to her. "You're wrong about something else too." He gave her the envelope.

"This is something I want you to see."

Slowly, she opened the envelope. Nothing could have prepared her for what she was about to see. There were two photographs. In the first picture was a beautiful young lady with dark, curly brown hair and expressive brown eyes sitting on a boulder near a pond. A large, black dog was by her side. The second was a dark and blurred picture of what looked to be the same young lady walking in the woods at night.

"My source sent me that," Chief Sengj spoke, his deep voice caring.

Ajahadé looked up at him, "I—Is this who I think it is?" She bit her bottom lip trying to contain the emotions that were threatening to appear. *Is this really Chrystalia—my baby girl?*

"Yes, it's Chrystalia," he said. "She is alive."

Without warning, streams of tears came flooding out of Ajahade's eyes. "Sh—she made it!? My baby—she's alive?"

"Yes," Chief Sengj responded, clearing his throat.

Gently, Ajahadé brushed her finger across the image of Chrystalia's face. "I—I just can't believe it."

"I couldn't either. We knew she had made it to the United States but after that, she went cold and I anticipated the worse."

Ajahadé nodded. "Where is she? Where was this?"

"That," he pointed to the first picture, "was taken in North Carolina but unfortunately, she ran off into the woods and my source lost her." He paused and pointed to the second picture. "She later saw Chrystalia in the woods at night and snapped the second picture, but unfortunately, lost her again."

"But she's in North Carolina."

"She was then, yes."

"When was this?"

"Several weeks ago." He paused. "My source is still trying to find her but hasn't seen her again."

Ajahadé nodded and continued looking at the picture. Several moments passed before either spoke. Chief Sengj was the first, "And that's where I need your help." His voice was quiet.

Ajahadé looked up. "Help to find her?"

Chief Sengj nodded. "She is alive but my gut is telling me something is wrong."

"How wrong?"

"Like she is in danger." Ajahade's entire body tensed. *This is my baby—the only one of my children who is still alive.* The longing to find her, to be with Chrystalia, was so strong she could barely think.

Instead, she nodded. "What about Ish?"

"I'll find him," Chief Sengj said confidently. "I just need you to find Chrystalia and make sure she is safe."

Ajahadé nodded. "Yes sir."

A small smile stretched across the serious man's face. "Very well, then. I'll have Jahdej take you to the training center, so you can brush up on your skills and learn about the US."

A look of confusion crossed Ajahade's face. *I've been to the United States several times–I don't think I need the cultural training again.*

"The US has changed a lot since you were there last," Chief Sengj explained, "and you'll need some more practice with their ways."

She nodded. "Okay."

LOCATION: UNITED STATES OF AMERICA
TIME: SEVERAL DAYS LATER

"You ready for this?" Chase asked several days later as he and Sarah walked down the long hallway within the retirement home.

Sarah smiled. "Yes, are you?"

"Absolutely," he said just as they entered the Activity Room. There were already about twenty senior residents inside waiting for them.

Sarah walked to the front of the room and checked to make sure the microphones and sound system were working properly before she spoke. "Hi everyone, today we are going to have a slightly different kind of music for you. I am going to play the piano and Chase is going to sing for us."

Everyone smiled and a few clapped. Sarah walked over to the piano and Chase took his position at the microphone. Looking at Chase, she started the introduction of the song. Though the piano was not as nice and was slightly out of tune, the melody was still pretty.

However, when Chase's majestic voice joined with the notes of the piano, the music was sent to an entirely different level: it was astonishing. Everyone grew still—not even the nurse who had been darting about the room checking on residents moved. The residents, who were able, slid to the edge of their seats in complete concentration. The sound was so beautiful, so heartfelt, and so smooth that it took their breath away.

When the song came to an end, the entire room burst into intense applause. By the energy of their claps, it was obvious they wanted to do a standing ovation but their bodies would not allow them to stand. Sarah and Chase both smiled and nodded their appreciation for the applause and then started the next song.

They had performed for nearly an hour when Sarah looked up to see a woman in a wheelchair entering the room, her wheelchair being pushed by a teenage girl. The girl pushed her grandmother into the room but the expression on the teenager's face was priceless: it was a look of shock and amazement.

Sarah looked over to see Chase watching the teenager as well. He looked at Sarah and gave her an expression that told her he was finished. She drew the song to a close. The room burst into vibrant applause. Chase walked over, grabbed Sarah's hand, and pulled her to the front. Bowing slightly to their applause, he smiled and led her out of the room.

With haste, he led her down the long hallway. "Are you okay, Chase?" she asked, unsure how to respond to his haste yet feeling her body tensing.

He turned and looked over his shoulder. "We'll see." He looked forward and then at Sarah. "What's the quickest and most inconspicuous way out of here?"

"Through the kitchen," Sarah responded and led him to the right. In just a few minutes, they were outside and in Chase's dark black SUV. Chase cranked the car almost instantly.

Chase and Sarah were both completely quiet as Chase quickly pulled the vehicle out of the parking lot and onto the road. He kept glancing in his rearview mirror as though looking for someone to follow them.

Sarah watched him but said nothing. The silence dragged on.

He took several turns and then another one. *He's going away from Dr. Mychael's house...*she thought as she watched. *Where is he going?* A knot of fear grew in her stomach as the situation grew similar to ones she'd had with Richard. She pushed down the feeling. *This is Chase, not Richard. He isn't going to hurt me.*

He took another turn and then another before he finally turned onto a road that looked familiar. *Okay, this road will take us to her house. He just went a very round-about way to get there.*

A few minutes later, he pulled up to the familiar gate, typed in a code and entered through the gates. He pulled his vehicle into the garage and turned it off. But he did not get out. Instead, he just sat there for a moment staring straight ahead as though deep in thought.

"Please," Sarah said, her voice quiet as her eyes watched his worried face, "please tell me what you're thinking, Chase."

He paused and took a deep breath. Then, keeping his gaze straight ahead he spoke, his voice quiet, "I screwed up."

Sarah looked confused. "What do you mean?"

"I screwed up. I—" he paused as though trying to find the words. "I should not have gone today."

"Why not? Everyone loved it."

"Yes, but it was not smart of me and now—now I regret it."

"Okay, Chase, you're going to have to explain it a little more because I still do not understand."

He took another deep breath and then turned to look at her, his blue eyes inundated with sadness and worry. "I'm not who you think I am," he paused. "Am I the person you met years ago? Yes. Am I the person I've been around you now? Yes. But I failed to tell you what I do for a living and that—" he paused, "that changes everything."

She looked at him, her eyes searching his face as she thought. *Are my speculations correct? Is Chase the musical artist CJ?*

She looked down and then back at him before she spoke, her voice barely above a whisper. "Are," she stuttered, "are you CJ?"

A look of shock and somewhat relief washed over his face. "You already knew?"

She shook her head. "No, but I suspected. I'd heard your voice on the cassette tapes that you sent me years ago, so when I heard songs being played at restaurants, I recognized the voice but wasn't sure. It just didn't add up. I knew you had the talent in you, but when I looked at the showman on stage in front of millions of people, he did not seem like the same person I knew." She paused. "But there was something about CJ's music that drew me in and calmed my spirit. It helped me get by."

Chase looked deep in thought as he processed what she had just said. For a long moment, there was silence between them. Then he spoke, "Yes, that's me. And I'm glad that the songs helped you. Several were written when I was thinking about you."

A look of shock and amazement washed over Sarah's face. "Really?"

"Yes, especially the song 'You Are Gone.'" He paused. "I wrote that one shortly after I stopped hearing from you."

For a moment, Sarah was quiet. Feelings and thoughts whirled around inside her mind as she realized that the song that had helped her get through the hard times was actually written about her. *He loved me then just like he does now. That song aches with pain of losing someone he loved and it shows that losing each other so many years ago hurt him just as much as it did me.*

"I–I" she stuttered, "I can't believe that. That was the song that helped me get by. It helped calm my fears and everything."

A sheepish smile washed over Chase's face as he

reached over to hold her hand. "I'm so glad."

She smiled back. "But tell me, how did it happen? How did you go from the guy I knew at camp to CJ?"

"Things just sort of happened. I went to college and started getting a degree. While I was there, I stumbled into a professor who took me under his wings and taught me a lot. He ended up telling a talent-spotter about me. That spotter came to one of my recitals and then offered me an incredible recording contract. I went to California and from there, I worked hard on my music career."

Sarah nodded in understanding. "And is that why you had so much security at the hospital?"

"Yes, fans get out of control. If they'd known where I was, we would have been flooded with paparazzi; I wanted to recover in peace. So security was there both to protect us and to keep me out of sight from the public eye."

Sarah nodded. "Okay, that's making more sense now."

Chase nodded. "Good." For another moment, there was silence as Sarah processed the information. He then spoke, "Is there anything else you want to know? I'm all open. Anything you want to know."

"What about the accident? What happened?"

"I was practicing a stunt for my concert in Germany where I'm held by an almost invisible line and raised above the crowd. The line snapped and I crashed onto the stage below, breaking my legs, etc."

Sarah's thought for a minute before she responded, "Wow. What about the burns?"

"There were flames coming up from the sides of the platform I was standing on and when I fell, the flames got out of hand."

"Wow," she responded. "That's awful."

He nodded. "Yeah, but I made it. I had to cancel the world tour but my lawyers are on it and they think I'll be able to get a lot of compensation for the financial damages that happened."

"Why haven't I heard about this in the news?"

"My lawyers and the lawyers of the company in charge of the stunts have asked for silence about it until the investigation is completed. So the media is in the dark about it right now. They just know I canceled the tour due to 'personal reasons' and will be back at a later date."

Sarah nodded. "I'd seen that in the news but didn't put two-and-two together."

Chase nodded. "Yeah, I'm trying to keep it as low-key as possible. That's also why I came here. This way I can spend time with Grandmamma and be virtually hidden from the media's eye."

"That makes sense," she paused, "and it also explains that teenager's reaction when she saw you this afternoon."

"Yes, exactly," Chase responded, his voice matter-of-fact. "She recognized me. I didn't think the older folks would recognize me, which was why I offered in the first place. For some reason, the thought did not occur to me that there might be younger people there who would recognize me."

"Yeah, there are usually some younger people there visiting their families."

"Yeah, makes sense, but I just didn't think about it. So, when I saw her face, it occurred to me what I'd done. Not only had I revealed myself here so the media may come, but I also endangered you because now they are going to connect us to one another. All it takes is for that girl to take a picture, post it on social media, and the rest is history."

Suddenly, the reality of the situation hit Sarah. She realized that her cover was most likely blown and Richard—should he be watching the TV or searching online—would quickly find out her whereabouts. This was especially true given the fact that his people were probably already in this area if the girl with the Scottish terrier had been his spotter. Fear raised its ugly head, and for a moment she was breathless. *I have to get out of here. I have to leave.*

"Sarah, please tell me what you are thinking." Chase's tone of voice was soft and laden with vulnerability. "Are you mad?"

She shook her head. "No, I'm not mad. I'm just

evaluating the situation and the risks involved in it. This could be big."

"Yes, it could be. I'm going to hope she didn't take pictures—it didn't look like she did. I think we left in time, but I'm not sure. Either way, I'm hoping she didn't." He scratched his head.

"Me too."

"Sarah," Chase paused. "Do you think Richard is still looking for you?"

Sarah nodded. "Yes, I—I know he is. He won't stop until he gets his way with me."

"Okay, then let's do this. With your permission, I'll assign some of my bodyguards to take care of you. You can stay here at Grandmamma's place so that you're safe behind the fence and gate. Then, if you want to go out, the bodyguards can go with you."

Sarah thought for a moment. *That may work for a little while...*but there was a feeling bubbling up inside of her—it was a feeling of restlessness and desperation to leave. Fighting it, she responded to Chase, "Thanks."

"What else could I do to help you be safe?"

Sarah thought for another moment. "I'm not sure."

"Grandmamma's fence has sensors and cameras on it. I haven't had them all turned on, but I'll turn them on now. That way, if anyone comes close to the fence, we'll know and we'll also be able to see who it is."

When Sarah nodded, he asked, "You have a cell phone—do you have my number on speed dial?"

"No, but I will."

"Okay, and here—" he reached into his back pocket and pulled out his cell phone, "let me get you the name and number of my security leader. That way, if you need anything, he can get it for you to make sure you're safe."

Sarah took the number and put it into her phone. "Thanks, Chase."

"Sure," he paused and she could tell he was thinking hard, "I'm not sure what else I can do..." his voice trailed off. "Oh, I know, I'll just talk to my security lead and see what he suggests. This is his area of expertise, so I'll just talk to him."

Sarah nodded, her mind still buzzing with all that had just transpired.

Chase reached over and gently grabbed her hand. "Sarah." He paused and waited for her to look at him, "I can't tell you how sorry I am about this. I don't know what I was thinking. I should have known better."

"Chase," she paused and gently rubbed his hand, "it'll be okay. You didn't do this intentionally and I was just as much a part of this as you were. I could have said something."

"But you didn't know who I was..." He let the sentence hang.

"I didn't know for sure but I suspected. It would have been smart of me to confirm before I allowed myself to be seen in public with you."

"Don't blame yourself, Sarah. This was me."

Sarah looked hesitant but slowly nodded. "We'll figure this out."

"Yes, we will," he said.

The feeling inside of her continued to grow…she felt restless and wanted to run. *Think,* she told herself, *don't feel, just think about what you need to do right now….* Then another feeling grew strong. *I want to go home. I want to be at home, with Zeus, so I can think and figure out my next move.*

"I'm going to go home," Sarah said, somewhat abruptly. "I need to get some things and think about this."

"I can go with you."

Sarah shook her head. "No, I need to go by myself so I can think. If that girl posted a picture already, it'll take time before Richard finds it and comes here, so I'll be okay."

Chase looked hesitant. "But I don't like the idea of you being by yourself when there's such a threat right now."

"But the more we are out in public together, the more likely this will be publicized even more."

Chase looked thoughtful as he evaluated her point. "You're right." He paused. "Okay, how about this? You go home and get Zeus and your stuff. I'll stay here and contact my security and handle those arrangements—including bumping up the security and surveillance here. By the time you get back, everything should be set."

"Okay," Sarah said, her mind still spinning like a whirlwind.

"Let me call one of the security personnel and get them to go with y—"

"No," Sarah said, cutting him off, "I'll be okay." Again, Chase looked hesitant but she insisted. "I'll be fine, Chase. I've made it this long by myself, so I can do it again, and I need some space to figure out how to handle this."

The look of worry and concern grew stronger on his face but slowly he nodded. "Okay, just please make sure you have your phone on you at all times. It's fully charged, right?"

"Yes," she said, "It was charging on the way here."

"Okay, and make sure you call the police and me if anything seems odd." She nodded. "And let me know when you are on your way back over here."

Again, she nodded. "I love you, Chase," she said, her voice quiet and serious.

"I love you too, Sarah," he said, gently pulling her hand

up. Kissing it, he pulled his blue eyes up to meet her brown ones. "Please promise me that you'll be careful."

"I will."

LOCATION: UNITED STATES OF AMERICA

His steps were determined as he walked towards the local bar. Once inside, he sat down and ordered a drink. He sat for a few minutes and then put his head down on the bar in front of him. "You alright, man?" the bartender asked.

"Naw," Richard responded. "Tryin' to find my daughter but can't."

"Runaway?"

"Yep," he responded and took another gulp of beer. "Can't find her. Someone told me that she may be here but I've been here for days and can't find 'er yet."

"What does she look like?"

Richard reached into his pocket and pulled out a picture of Sarah as a teenager. "That's her as a teenager. She's in her twenties now."

"Haven't seen her since then?"

"Nope."

"Why you searching for her now?" the bartender asked frankly. "A girl gone that long probably doesn't want to be found."

Instantly, anger flared up in Richard and he stood up ready to fight. "Whoa!" the bartender said, holding up his hand. "I don't want no trouble, man. No need for that here."

With clenched teeth, Richard slowly moved away from the bartender and sat back down to continue drinking.

CHAPTER NINE

"Hey buddy. Hey," Sarah said to Zeus, who was wagging his tail excitedly. "Good to see you too." She rubbed his back. His normal behavior calmed her nerves slightly. *He acts like everything is normal, so hopefully nothing suspicious happened here.*

She closed and locked the door. Then she walked through the house, looking into every closet and place a person could hide. *Okay, all clear.* She sat down on the couch. Zeus walked over to her and gently placed his head on her knee. *Even Zeus can tell something is wrong,* she thought.

For several long minutes, she reviewed the incident at the retirement home in her mind and began evaluating the situation. *I introduced us to the crowd at the beginning of the hour, but that girl wasn't there. However, everyone there knows me, so all she had to do is ask her grandmother who I was and then tag me in a picture.* Quickly, she reached for her phone and

151

began searching online. For a long time, she searched before she located a small tweet that mentioned seeing CJ at a retirement home. *Okay, so far no mention of me....* But her thoughts were cut off just as something else popped up on the screen. Her heart plummeted to the floor. There on her phone was an image of Chase standing in the activity room, and in the background, she saw her own face. *I'm done.*

The feeling of fear that had been growing all night grew exponentially—it grabbed her throat and almost all of her breath dissipated. *Breathe,* she told herself, *you've got to think about this logically.* But the feeling was so strong. *I can't. I love Chase so much...what if Richard sees this and goes after Chase thinking Chase will lead him to me.* The thought was unbearable. *I cannot endanger Chase. He is so wonderful. I love him. I would never forgive myself if anything happened to him.*

The feeling of restlessness and fear became overwhelming. *I've got to escape. I've got to get out of here.* Without another thought, she succumbed to her feelings and began to follow her plan of escape. With rehearsed movements, she picked up several things and burned them in the fireplace then walked through the house to cover up any signs of her escape, even placing her cell phone on the charger before gathering a few meager belongings. She put them into a backpack, and—with Zeus by her side—she vanished into the night.

LOCATION: PACIFIC ISLANDS
TIME: SEVERAL DAYS LATER

"Your kicking is amazing," Jhava said to Ajahadé who was covered in sweat and breathing hard. "Great power, form, and precision–just as Chief had always told us."

Ajahadé smiled as she wiped a stream of sweat off her face. "Good."

"Now, let's fire some shots."

Ajahadé nodded and followed the huge, muscular Chaitian to a lane in the indoor shooting range. Within a few minutes, she had on ear protection and was firing shots at the target that was suspended a long distance away.

When she'd finished firing a round of shots, she put down the gun, retrieved the target, and took off her ear muffs. Looking up, she saw a look of shock on Jhava's face. "Wow," was all he managed to say for several minutes.

Again, a small smile stretched across Ajahade's face as she waited for the trainer to gather his thoughts. After a few moments, he cleared his throat and spoke, "Okay, so that's true as well. I've never seen someone fire with so much accuracy at such a distance. It's like you were a sniper."

"Does that mean I'm ready for the next part of the test?" Ajahadé asked.

Jhava nodded and led her towards another part of the training facility. Here her skills would be put to the test in a real life-like scenario. She would be given the objective to save a hostage within a house. She would have to go through the house, shooting at mannequins of enemies that would pop up at her unexpectedly. If she shot one wrong mannequin, she would fail the test. If she managed to navigate the scenario successfully by shooting all the enemy targets and successfully obtaining the hostage, she would pass her final test of the tactical training.

She entered the house and a few minutes later emerged to see Jhava sporting his now-expected look of shock. "You managed to do that test successfully and broke our time record doing it." He paused. "I have nothing to teach you."

Ajahadé nodded and then walked out of the room. A few minutes later, she entered the office of a young American-looking man who was sitting behind a desk typing on a computer. "May I help you?" the man asked, without looking up, as she entered.

"Chief Sengj told me to report to you for my cultural training," Ajahadé responded, her gaze on his desk and away from his eyes.

He looked up and instantly recognized her. "Ajahadé," he said, his voice full of respect, and she nodded. "Sure, sit down."

She sat down in the chair opposite of his desk and listened as he filled her in on the American way of life. *I know so much of this already,* she thought to herself.

"One of the main things, though, is you've got to remember to make eye contact with everyone. If you don't, they will think you are shy and timid, which will weaken any points you try to make."

Ajahadé nodded. "I remember that."

"Okay, good." He paused and turned to get something out of his desk. "Another thing is technology. They have a lot of new technology they didn't have last time you were there, so you'll want to make sure you know the basics." He handed her a tablet and smart phone. "Feel free to take these with you and play with them. Just leave them in your room when you head out and the staff will make sure they get back to me."

Ajahadé took the devices and nodded her thanks. "Is there anything else?"

The American shook his head. "Nope. I'll sign off on your papers that you've done this and—Jhava tells me you passed the physical test—so we'll make sure Chief gets these. You can meet with him any time now, and he can give you his orders."

Ajahadé nodded just as images of Chrystalia came before her mind. *I am coming for you, my baby girl. Mum is almost ready to depart.*

LOCATION: CHAITI

As the clouds slowly stretched across the moon, concealing its light, the night turned darker. Even the animals of the forest grew quiet as dark figures made their way silently through the woods. They slowly entered a clearing and looked down at the humble hut below.

Like wolves circling their prey, they surrounded the hut. Drawing their weapons, they waited for the cue from their leader. With one quick look, the leader cast his signal and the entire group burst into the small hut, guns pointed and ready to fire. To their surprise, Ajahade's hut was void any sign of life.

"She's got to be hiding something," one of the Mashottiís said between clenched teeth. "Look hard!"

The group of men scoured every inch of the place. With violent movements, they grabbed each of her belongings, looked at them closely, and—when failing to find anything—threw everything to the ground, smashing them to pieces.

"There's nothing here, sir," one of the men said to their leader.

"I know, idiot!" he screamed. "Burn it." He stormed out of the hut. A few moments later, the entire hut was covered in flames just as the clouds above burst into rain.

LOCATION: PACIFIC ISLANDS
TIME: THE NEXT DAY

With Chief Sengj's permission, Ajahadé entered his dark office and sat down on the big leather chair in the corner. For a moment, both of them were quiet. Finally, the diplomat spoke, his deep voice serious, "Okay, Aj, the time has come."

Ajahade's face was serious as she responded, "Yes sir. It has."

"My men tell me you're back to your old self."

Ajahadé shook her head. "I'm not as young as before so not as good, but I'm good enough."

Chief Sengj smiled and nodded his head. "Okay, there are a few things you should know before you leave." He paused and sat down on the chair near hers. "My contact has not been able to spot Chrystalia anymore. She is uncertain if Chrystalia is still anywhere in that area or not. However, I recommend still going because there are some people who may know her, and it's our best lead so far."

Ajahadé nodded.

"I'll give you everything that my contact has told me but I cannot give her contact information to you because I've put her on another assignment far from there." He paused again. "The second thing is that the Mashottiís have taken your hut. They destroyed it last night."

There was a flash of emotion across Ajahade's face

before it went emotionless. "Another sign my gut was correct."

Chief Sengj nodded. "Which is why I trust your instincts and have total faith that you can find my granddaughter." His face grew serious. "Look." She met his gaze and he continued, "I have utmost confidence in your ability to find her and bring her home safely." He shifted his weight in his seat. "It is also important for you to know that you still have diplomatic immunity in that country. That said, I don't want a large body count, so please, stay low and just get her to safety as fast as possible without making a big scene."

Ajahade's face was serious as she responded, "I'll do my best, sir."

"Very well," he said and stood up. Reaching into his desk drawer, he pulled out a large envelope. "In here is all the information you need. I am going to get Yahja, one of my agents, to go with you. She'll meet you in the lobby." Ajahadé nodded, took the envelope, and stood up to leave.

She turned back. "Chief?"

"Yes."

"May I ask if we have received any word about my brother and Jarah?"

She saw as the diplomat slowly shook his head. "No, but I have good people on it, and they will figure out what happened to them."

Ajahadé nodded her head and left his office without saying another word.

LOCATION: UNITED STATES OF AMERICA

"Something is wrong, Grandmamma," Chase said as he paced back and forth in the kitchen. "She told me she would tell me when she was coming back, and it's been too long."

"She needs time to gather her thoughts," Dr. Mychael responded calmly. "How long has it been?"

Chase looked at his phone. "Three hours."

Dr. Mychael looked thoughtful for a moment. "Hm, that is quite a while, but maybe it just took her a bit to think and to pack up all her stuff if she is going to be here for a while."

Chase continued pacing. "But this long? Maybe she needs help packing." He sighed. "I wish she'd let me go with her. This is killing me."

"Have you called her?"

"I texted her but she didn't answer." He pulled out his phone. "Let me try calling her and see if she answers." He dialed her number and listened to it ring over and over until finally her voicemail message came on. He left a message and then hung up.

"Not answering..." Dr. Mychael said, stating the obvious.

"Nope," Chase said and then began pacing again. "I—I just have this bad feeling in my stomach, Grandmamma. Like something is going on with her."

"Then go," Dr. Mychael said confidently. "Trust your gut. Maybe something is wrong and she needs you."

"But she didn't want me to come because she thought it'd give more attention."

"Wear a disguise, dear," Dr. Mychael said and then walked over to the closet. She pulled out a wig, hat, and sunglasses. Chase put them on.

"Thanks, Grandmamma. I'll let you know what happens. Make sure you answer the phone." She nodded and he walked out the door.

LOCATION: ASHVILLE, NC

His presence was intimidating as he stood next to the grocery store counter waiting for an answer.

"Yeah, we've seen a girl like that," the lanky man from behind the counter said to Richard. "She comes in here regularly but doesn't talk much."

"What days does she come?"

"Hm, I'm not sure—lemme ask Gloria," the man said and yelled to another cashier.

"She usually comes in on Monday," Gloria responded and walked over towards Richard and the other cashier. "She doesn't usually buy much but always gets a sandwich from the deli."

Richard nodded and listened as Gloria told him what Sarah drove. A deceitful smile stretched across his face as he left the grocery store.

LOCATION: SARAH'S HOUSE

"Sarah?" Chase said as he rang the doorbell another time and paused to listen for movement. "It's me, Chase." Again, there was no sound. He knocked on the door very hard and waited. No sound.

He stepped away from the door and walked around the house to the back door. Peeking into the windows, he could see that there were no lights on inside the house. *It's dark–if she were here packing, she would have the lights on.*

A bad feeling in his gut, he slowly walked up to the sliding glass door. He pulled the door, and to his surprise, it opened.

"Sarah?" he called as he walked into the house. Again, no sounds could be heard. He flipped on the light. *No Zeus,* he thought as the feeling inside his stomach grew stronger. He walked through the house. There was no sign of her.

Growing breathless, he pulled out his phone and dialed his grandmother. "She's not here," he said as soon as the older woman answered. "Sarah is not here."

"Any signs of forced entry?" Dr. Mychael's voice showed her concern.

"Not that I saw but the sliding glass door was unlocked."

"Strange," Dr. Mychael said. "Anything messed up inside her house?"

"No, everything looks normal."

For a few moments, there was silence as Dr. Mychael processed what was going on. "Okay, how about this. Why don't you go to her work and see if she went there. I don't know why she would go there at this time of night, but it doesn't hurt to look. Maybe she forgot something earlier."

"Okay," Chase said and then walked out of the house.

A few minutes later, he pulled up to the gate. Typing in the code Dr. Mychael had told him, he watched as the iron gate slowly opened and allowed his big black SUV to enter. He pulled through and waited for it to close behind him.

He parked in the parking lot near the main facility. Walking up to the door, he discovered that it was locked. He knocked for several minutes, but no one answered. He went to another door but again, no one answered. *It's too late at night,* he thought and got back inside his car.

"It's locked," he said into the phone. "I'm going to call the police."

"No," Dr. Mychael said, her voice firm. "Not yet. Come back here and get me."

Chase hesitated but respected his grandmother enough to obey. Hanging up with her, he steered his vehicle towards her house.

<><

"Her car is still here," Dr. Mychael said as they pulled into Sarah's driveway a little while later.

Chase nodded. "Which is why I thought she was still home when I got here." Dr. Mychael nodded. A few minutes later, they were inside her house.

Methodically, Dr. Mychael walked through Sarah's house, inspecting everything in it. "Everything looks normal in the dining room and kitchen," she said and walked toward the living room. She approached the fireplace. "Chase, do you see this?"

He came over and stood beside her. "Something was burned in here recently."

"You're right," she said and they both looked over the fireplace thoroughly.

"I wonder what..." Chase's voice trailed off.

Dr. Mychael walked to the bedroom. Once in there, she instantly noticed the cell phone. "That explains why she isn't answering her phone."

Chase nodded. "And she promised me that she'd keep it on her at all times." He paused as the feeling in his stomach grew worse. "Grandmamma, do you think she was taken?"

Dr. Mychael looked serious. "I'm not sure. She could have been taken, but she also could have left on her own. She's done it before."

Chase nodded and thought hard for several long minutes. "The tapes," he said frankly. "Where are the tapes...."

"What do you mean?"

"Sarah kept the tapes I sent her when we were younger. If she left on her own accord, I know she wouldn't leave without them. She told me that she would never leave them behind."

"Okay," Dr. Mychael responded. "Do you know where she kept them?"

"Somewhere in her bedroom," he said. "She told me she still had them in her bedroom but did not say where."

"Then let's see if we can find those tapes."

After over an hour of searching, Chase finally stated the obvious, "They are not here."

"I agree," Dr. Mychael said. "So that's probably a good sign."

Chase looked hesitant and then walked out of the room. He walked through the house and outside on the back patio. That's when he noticed it: Sarah's bicycle was missing. *She left on her bicycle so that people would not trace her by her car. Smart. But a bicycle would not get her very far and it isn't fast. She may still be in the area.*

"Grandmamma?" Chase yelled in the house. A few

moments later, the older woman appeared. "Sarah's bicycle is gone."

"She must have left on it," the older woman paused, "which means she may not be too far from here, although–" she paused, "it's been several hours. She could be quite far."

"True, but not as far as we were thinking," Chase responded and pulled out his phone. "I got a text saying that my security team is at your place, so I'll put them on to the task. We can all search this area."

Dr. Mychael looked serious. "How much do you trust them?"

"I trust them some, why?"

"Because you will have to instruct them *not* to post Sarah's picture online and other places because that will be very dangerous for her–you'll have to trust that they will comply. Otherwise, this search will do more harm than good."

Chase looked thoughtful for several moments before he responded, his voice serious, "That's true. I didn't think of it like that. We are going to have to be careful."

"Indeed."

CHAPTER TEN

"Ma'am, would you like a drink?" the flight attendant said to Ajahadé as she walked past Ajahade's row on the commercial airplane.

Ajahadé shook her head. "No thanks," she said in English. The woman nodded and moved the cart to the next row.

Shifting her weight, Ajahadé continued to stare out the window as her mind wandered toward Chrystalia and the task ahead. *Where are you, my little girl?* Ajahadé thought as the image of Chrystalia came back into her mind. *And how am I going to find you?*

Then, bit by bit, she constructed her plan and—by the time the flight landed—she was ready. Taking her bag from overhead and making eye contact with Yahja, they exited the plane.

"My luggage, ma'am," Yahja said in Chaitian just as a

large strain of her dark black hair fell across of her face.

"Okay," Ajahadé said in English and walked toward baggage claim. "Remember though, no Chaitian or French here, Yahja. Only use English lest we stand out."

Realization washed over the young woman's face as she realized what she had just done. "I'm so sorry ma'am," she said, looking clearly upset.

Without showing emotion, Ajahadé replied, "It's fine. Just don't do it again."

The other lady nodded and followed Ajahadé to baggage claim. A little while later, they were in a rental car and heading towards the hotel.

"What is our plan, ma'am?" Yahja asked.

Ajahadé glanced over at her from the driver's seat. "We're going to the hotel tonight and getting a good night's sleep. Then we'll head out in the morning."

"Where to?"

"North Carolina," Ajahadé said, her voice indicating that was all she wanted to say right now. The younger woman opened her mouth to speak but slowly closed it when she saw the older woman's facial expression. Instead, she slid down in her seat and watched out the window.

<><

The light was dim from the single lamp Ajahadé had left

on. Sitting on the couch within the hotel suite, she slowly took out the contents of the package that Chief Sengj had given her. Inside had been her passport and other important documentation, but there were also the two pictures and a document with the information that his source had given him.

Ajahadé slowly began reading. With each sentence, her heart yearned more and more to see the young woman the source described. Though the information was quite scarce—simply the locations where the two photographs were taken and a list of places that the source had searched without success—Ajahadé read it over and over, knowing that somehow those small pieces of information would help her.

After a while, she sat back and thought about Chrystalia. *Such a sweet child...she always loved animals, so it makes sense that she would have a dog. In fact, judging by how much she loved to horseback ride with me, it is no surprise that she got such a huge dog that's nearly the size of a small horse. And that may be my main lead. A small-framed woman like her paired with a huge black dog would certainly stand out. When I ask around Asheville, I will be sure to mention the dog....*

"Ma'am?" a quiet, feminine voice said from the shadows. "Is everything okay?"

"Yes, Yahja. You can go back to bed."

"Is there anything I can help with?"

"Not right now. Thank you, though." Ajahadé said

simply and watched as the other woman went back to bed.

A few minutes later, Ajahadé slowly put the contents back into the envelope and walked towards the bed. Putting the envelope underneath her pillow, she fell asleep.

LOCATION: ASHEVILLE, NORTH CAROLINA, USA

"I'm at a loss," Chase said sluggishly to Dr. Mychael after nearly forty-eight hours of non-stop searching. "I don't know where else to look."

"Honey," Dr. Mychael responded, her voice so tired it was hoarse, "we've done all that we can do for right now. Let's just go home, get a good night's rest and see what we can do tomorrow."

Chase slowly nodded and turned his vehicle towards their home. A few minutes later, they entered the house and he crashed onto his bed.

But—despite his exhaustion—his sleep was not peaceful. Instead, the images of Sarah with her expressive brown eyes and beautiful curly hair kept flashing before his eyes. He dreamed she was being hurt by Richard and yet he was powerless to defend her against Richard's evil blows. Suddenly, Chase woke up breathless.

Rolling over, he looked outside and into the night. "Sarah, where are you, my love? I want to know that you are safe," he whispered.

He heard the floor creak and looked up to see a shadow in the shape of Dr. Mychael in the doorway. She walked inside and sat down on his bed. For a moment, they both looked out at the night sky and said nothing. Finally, Dr. Mychael spoke, her voice low and loving. "She's not going to be found unless she wants to be found."

"What do you mean?"

"I mean," she paused, "this is not the first time she has vanished. She vanished from Richard before and went zigzagging across the country to flee him. And—despite the fact that all he wanted to do in his life was to find her—he did not find her. I suspect she'll be doing the same thing now and—unless she wants us to find her— we won't. She's that good."

For a moment, there was complete silence as Chase processed and evaluated what his grandmother had just said. "That makes sense, Grandmamma," he paused. "But, I can't just sit here knowing that she may be in danger and not at least try to find her. I mean, I lost her before and it killed me—it was like there was this gap in me where she belonged. She is the love of my life, and I cannot bear the thought of not having her."

A small stream of tears trickled down Dr. Mychael's wrinkled face. "I know." She swallowed hard. "She's been like a granddaughter to me. I feel like she is one of my own. The way she has taken care of me...." Her voice trailed off. "I love her too."

Chase leaned towards his nightstand and pulled a tissue out of the box. He gave it to his grandmother.

"Thank you," she responded and he nodded.

"I just wish I knew she was okay," he said. "The not knowing is killing me."

Dr. Mychael slowly patted her face with the tissue. "Me too. I just want to know that she is safe.

LOCATION: CHAITI

Covered by darkness, the men circled the hut like wolves circling their prey. This time, part of the group pointed their weapons towards the hut while the others walked quietly towards the entrance.

They disappeared into the hut and emerged a few moments later, a bound and beaten Bahja in their possession. The leader looked at the group and gave his signal. With haste, they all fired their guns at the hut until one of them threw a grenade into it. The entire hut blew up and burst into flames.

<><

"You will tell me what you know and you will tell me now!" an angered Mashottii screamed, in French, to Bahja who had been taken to a Mashottiian building and suspended from the ceiling by his hands. His feet were also bound.

The older man pulled his beard-covered lips tighter together, indicating he would tell them nothing. Bahja would not betray his promise to Ajahadé to keep her escape from the country a secret.

The Mashottií grew angrier. Picking up an iron bar, he slammed it against Bahja's side. He screamed in pain and the Mashottií hit again. Finally, he stopped and approached Bahja again. "Look," his deep voice was filled with anger while his beady eyes darted around Bahja's weathered face, "we know you know Ajahadé, and we know you helped her to escape. Tell us where she went."

The older man, again, drew his lips tighter. The Mashottií hit him again. He wrenched in pain but still refused to speak.

"Okay, if you won't tell us *where* she went, tell us *why* she went. Does she know anything about Steliana?"

Again, the older man refused. He was beaten again and again but never spoke a single word. His loyalty to his country was until death: he died by the hand of the Mashottiís.

LOCATION: UNITED STATES OF AMERICA

"Are you hungry?" Ajahadé asked the younger woman as they drove down the highway.

"No," the younger woman responded. "Where are we going?"
"Asheville." Ajahadé said simply.

"Do you think she is there?"

"I'm not sure but I hope so," Ajahadé said, her voice showing little emotion.

"Look," the younger lady said, her voice serious, "I get the feeling you don't like me. What did I do?"

"You didn't do anything; I don't dislike you. I just get quiet when I'm on a mission and when I'm trying to learn someone." She paused and glanced over at the younger woman, "I don't trust quickly."

"Why not?"

"I've learned the hard way that trusting quickly can be dangerous. Just give me some time and let me learn you can be trusted."

The younger lady swallowed. "Okay," was all she managed to say and then turned back to look out the window.

Several hours later, they arrived in Asheville. Ajahadé took several turns and went down a long, country road. After several miles, she slowed down and turned into a parking lot. She parked the car and they both got out.

"Where are we?" Yahja asked.

"The park where she was spotted," Ajahadé said simply as she walked towards a trail. When she got to the edge of the parking lot, she bent down and removed her shoes. Walking barefoot in the woods, she followed the trail.

After walking for several miles, the women entered a clearing. In the clearing was a pond with large rocks and boulders surrounding. *This is it–this is where the picture was taken.* Ajahadé walked around the pond until she could locate the angle from which the picture was taken. *It was taken right here, which means Chrystalia was on that rock.*

Ajahadé walked to the other side of the pond and pulled herself up onto the rock. Yahja followed. "This is beautiful," Yahja said.

"Sure is," Ajahadé responded. *I can see why Chrystalia was here.*

"Do you think this is where the picture was taken?"

Ajahadé nodded. "Yep. She was sitting right here."

There were a few moments of silence as Ajahadé listened to the sounds of nature. Finally, she stood up. "Okay, let's look around and see if we can find anything."

"What are we looking for?"

"Anything that can help us find her." The younger woman nodded and followed Ajahadé through the woods. After a while, they ended up back at the car with empty hands.

"Do you like dogs?" Ajahadé asked as soon as they were back in the vehicle.

"Yes, my family had one."

"Okay, well, we're going to need that knowledge. We're going to a pet store to see what we can find out." Yahja nodded.

LOCATION: ASHEVILLE, UNITED STATES OF AMERICA
ONE WEEK AFTER DISAPPEARANCE

Just as the sun was peeking over the horizon, Chase woke. Turning over, he watched a small bird land on the tree outside his window before flying off towards the sunrise. An aroma of bacon filled his room. Scratching his sleep-deprived eyes, he slowly slid out of bed and followed the smell towards the massive kitchen. There his grandmother stood, skillfully cooking breakfast. She heard him enter and looked up from the pan where she was stirring scrambled eggs. "Good morning," she said.

"Can I help with anything?" he asked. The older woman shook her head so he walked over to the bar and pulled up a stool. "Anything change since last night?"

Again, Dr. Mychael shook her head. "But I think it may be a good idea to go back to the retirement home today and see if anyone has heard anything."

Chase nodded. "I agree. I was planning to do that as soon as the doors open. I think I'll do my usual rounds and see if anyone knows."

Dr. Mychael nodded and glanced down at his leg, which was now only supported by a brace. "How much longer until you have to get back into the limelight?"

Chase looked distant. "I'm not going back until I find her safe and sound." Dr. Mychael opened her mouth to respond but—upon seeing his expression—she knew he could not be swayed. Instead, she stayed silent for several long minutes until breakfast was ready.

<><

"Mr. Two?" Chase said as he knocked on the familiar door. "Are you awake?"

"Yes, son, com'on in," the older man said in his thick Southern accent. Chase walked into his room. "Ya can shut the door behind ya, if ya want." Chase nodded and shut the door before sitting down on the chair in Mr. Two's living room.

"My wife's gone to get some breakfast from the kitchen, so I've got a few minutes with ya." He shifted his weight in his recliner and looked at Chase. "What can I help ya with?"

"I was just wondering if you've heard anything from Sarah?"

"Naw," the older man said, "but the soda guy—ya know, that kid—he's a little old boy, really, with black hair?" Chase shook his head, "Anyways, he's always had a bit of the googly eyes for her, but she always turned down that poor kid..." Mr. Two's voice drifted off and then he looked back up. "He wasn't her type anyway."

Chase nodded, unsure how to answer.

"Anyways," Mr. Two cleared his throat and then reached over to the small table beside his recliner and pulled open a drawer. Inside was a cola bottle. "The kid told me to make sure—and I quote–'make sure that singer guy gets this cola. It's for him, and only him.' And I told him okay, so here it is."

Chase looked confused but took the cola. "Well, thank you sir. I appreciate it. I don't know why he—"

"Who knows, son," Mr. Two interrupted, waving his hand. "Sometimes ya never know with kids these days."

Chase giggled. "Very true." About that time, Mrs. Two walked in the door and Chase politely excused himself.

Once out at his car, he inspected the cola thoroughly but saw nothing abnormal. *Why would a guy I don't even know send a soda to me?* Perplexed, he opened the cola; it fizzed like normal so he smelled it. Unsure if it was safe to drink—even though it had been sealed—he poured out a small fraction. *Normal color...*

But then he caught something. On the inside of the label, he saw what looked to be writing. Quickly, he poured out the rest of the soda and tried to read the writing. It was nearly impossible to read through the plastic bottle so he carefully removed the label. The writing was very small but clear enough that he could read it:

> *Chase,*
> *Follow the bottle to its giver but tell no one and come alone. I love you.*

There was no signature but he knew the handwriting without a doubt: it was Sarah. In her own amateur way, she was passing him an encoded message.

"Follow the bottle to its giver..." Chase said softly out loud. "So I have to find that kid that Mr. Two was talking about. Quickly, Chase put the wrapper in his pocket

and left his car.

Once inside the building, he went hastily to Mr. Two's door and knocked again. This time, Mr. Two answered the door. Once he saw who it was, he stepped out and pulled the door behind him. "What is it, son?"

"The cola guy who gave you this—what does he look like?"

"Welp," Mr. Two paused and scratched his head. "Lemme think how to describe 'em to ya…" He paused as he thought for a moment. "Welp, he is about your height, maybe a little shorter, and he's got big bulky arms—probably from liftin' all day."

Chase nodded. "Did you say he had black hair?"

"Yep, he's got black hair and I wanna say brown eyes—hold on." He turned and opened the door. "Honey, what color eyes do you think that little cola feller has?" He paused to listen. "The singer feller is tryin' to find him." He paused again. "Yeah. I don't know why, honey, just tell me! Does he have brown eyes?" He paused and then looked at Chase. "Yep, he's got brown eyes. He usually wears a blue shirt."

"Okay, thank you so much."

"Sure thing! He might even still be here—he was here a little while ago. Might wanna check the kitchen and see if he's there. If he ain't there, he'll be in the Activity Room down the hall because there's a drinking machine in there."

Chase nodded again and then vanished down the hallway.

<><

"Hey," Chase said a few minutes later as he spotted a young man refilling a soda machine.

The man looked up. "Hey."

"Are you–" and then it suddenly occurred to him that Mr. Two had not told him the guy's name. Before the silence could linger too long, the other man spoke.

"Are you Sarah's boyfriend, the singer?"

Chase nodded. "Yes."

"Did Mr. Two give you the soda?" Again, Chase nodded; a perplexed look was still on his face. The younger man nodded and then got closer. When he spoke, his voice was barely above a whisper. "Meet me at my truck in 5."

"Where is your truck?"

"Behind the cafeteria. The only soda truck out there." Chase nodded.

A few minutes later, Chase was standing outside the cafeteria near a bright blue soda truck when he saw the young man approaching, fork truck in tow. He put the fork truck in the back of the truck and walked around to Chase. Putting out his hand, he spoke, "I'm Brad."

Chase shook his hand. "Chase."

"Alright man, I need you to get in the truck with me."

"Why?"

His voice got quiet. "Got tell ya somethin' and can't tell ya here." Reluctantly, Chase obliged and climbed up into the truck.

Once they were both settled, Brad spoke. "K, so, what I'm supposed to tell ya—"

"Wait, no, just tell me the truth. Do you know where she is?"

Brad waved his hand. "Naw, but I can get ya closer to her." He paused. "She told me you'd be lookin' for her and that you'd go to Mr. Two. She told me to make sure to give that soda to him and tell him to make sure you got it."

Chase nodded. "But why do I need to be in your truck?"

"Because I'm going to take ya as close to 'er as I can get ya." He cranked the truck. "OH! I almost forgot. Ya gotta leave your phone."

"It's in my car," Chase said, "But why do I have to leave it?"

"I dunno, she told me to make sure you didn't have it. I 'spect so ya won't be tracked. Ready?"

Chase nodded and put on his seatbelt.

CHAPTER ELEVEN

LOCATION: CHAITI

The lighting was dark and the room cold as eight heavily armed men walked into the dark narrow office within the Mashottían headquarters. Inside sat a dark man, his evil eyes watching each man carefully as they walked—one at a time—into the office. Each man bowed and then stood still waiting for further instructions.

After several long moments of silence, the Mashottían leader turned to the last man inside the office and nodded his head. The other man closed and locked the door. Finally, the leader spoke, his deep voice laden with strictness and brutality.

"You have been hand-selected by me to fulfill an important task. That task is to find Steliana. She is vital to our war but vanished years ago. You must find her. But that is nearly impossible. We have searched with no success for years. Until now." He paused. "Now we have information we did not have then and it will lead us to her. Steliana has a daughter. This daughter will be able to tell us where Steliana is—she may not tell us quickly but with the right tactics," he paused as it became clear to each man that he was referring to torture, "she will bend and tell you what you need to know. I give you complete liberty to do what you wish to her as long as you get the information." He paused, "You get the information; then kill her. We'll have no use for her after that."

The men nodded and continued to listen for their immediate orders. Several hours later, they boarded a plane en route to the United States of America.

LOCATION: HOTEL IN ASHEVILLE, NC

"Thanks for your help, Yahja," Ajahadé said as they sat down in their hotel suite.

The other lady looked a bit puzzled. "I didn't do anything."

"Yes, you did actually. You talked to the ladies at the pet store."

"I was just being friendly. I didn't say anything meaningful."

"You didn't need to. The purpose was to get them comfortable with you so that the next time you go in there, they will recognize you and be more apt to tell us stuff."

The younger lady nodded as she walked over to her bag and pulled out a tablet. Sitting down on one of the beds, she began browsing the internet. Ajahadé on the other hand, flipped on the TV and sat down. Though she was facing the TV, it was obvious by her stare that she was not paying attention to it but was instead deep in thought. It was true that the ladies at the pet store had not said anything that was obviously helpful, but they had mentioned that a certain retired psychologist had been in the store earlier that week. Though they didn't say the psychologist's name, Ajahadé had a good feeling about who the older person had been and that, she reasoned was a good lead.

After several minutes, Yahja made a murmuring noise.

"What's that?" Ajahadé said and reached for the remote to turn down the TV.

"I looked up Asheville and apparently someone claims they saw CJ here a few weeks ago."

Ajahadé looked at her blankly. "Who's CJ?"

"He's a famous singer and pop star. I learned it in my Americanization training."

Ajahadé nodded. "And what do they say his reason was for being here?"

"They don't know; however, he has canceled his worldwide tour for 'personal reasons,' so they think his grandmother or grandfather may be dying," she paused, "because he was spotted in a nursing home."

Ajahadé nodded. "And this is important because—?" She let the sentence hang.

"Because of this picture," Yahja said and turned the tablet around so that Ajahadé could see what was on the screen. On it—though blurry—was a picture of CJ and in the background was a young lady with striking resemblance to Chrystalia sitting at the piano.

"Wow," Ajahadé said as she looked at the picture. "Can you zoom in?"

"Yes," Yahja said and put her fingers on the screen, "but it just gets blurrier."

"It's okay," Ajahadé replied and looked at the zoomed in

picture for several long minutes. "Though blurry, it really looks like her. Does it say which nursing home this was?"

"No, I looked and looked but can't find it. Someone said her name may be Sarah though."

Ajahadé nodded. "Okay, thanks." And with that she turned back to the TV and kept watching. She had acquired the information she needed.

After a while, Ajahadé picked up the tablet. She sat working on the tablet for over an hour before Yahja finally went to bed for the night.

D. L. Hays

LOCATION: MYCHAEL ESTATE

The moon was slowly becoming covered by clouds as the night grew darker. Dr. Mychael sat inside her library carefully considering what to do next. Now, not only was Sarah missing but Chase had not returned home. She highly suspected he was off chasing a lead but was still unsure.

Suddenly she heard a noise. It was far in the distance, but it sounded like a creak in the floor—as though someone was inside the house. Staying perfectly still on the dark leather seat, she waited. The sound happened again. This time it was closer to the library door.

Slowly and quietly, Dr. Michaels reached to the small table beside the chair and opened the drawer, revealing a pistol inside. Then, the sound happened again, but this time only a few feet away. Looking up, she saw the shadow of a small woman standing in front of her.

"Doc, it's me," a vaguely familiar and heavily accented voice said from the shadow. "Please don't shoot. I come in peace."

"Aj?" Dr. Mychael said, her voice showing her perplexity.

"Yes," the voice responded, in Chaitian.

Dr. Mychael reached over and turned on the lamp. The light instantly illuminated half of the room and gave her a full view of the intruder's face: indeed, it was Ajahadé.

"Ajahadé, my old friend," Dr. Mychael said in Chaitian and stood up to give her a hug. "I never thought I would see you again."

Ajahadé chuckled. "Everyone says that." She paused. "I think they thought I died."

"I thought you did," Dr. Mychael said and then pulled back from the embrace to inspect Ajahade's face. "You have more battle scars."

"Yes," Ajahadé said frankly. "I was tortured and left for dead."

"Let me guess. They wanted to know about your family."

Ajahadé nodded.

"Please," Dr. Mychael said, pointing to the chair beside her, "sit down."

Ajahadé nodded and sat down.

"How much time do you have?"

"Not much," Ajahadé responded. "Chief Sengj insisted that I bring an assistant, and I have left her asleep in the hotel."

Dr. Mychael laughed slightly. "Let me guess, she gets in the way more than she helps?"

Again, Ajahadé nodded. "Indeed."

"What brings you to the US, Aj? How did you get into my house—nevermind, I know that answer. Nothing stops you. But what brings you to my house?"

"My daughter," Ajahadé said frankly. "I only recently found out that she is alive and I have a gut feeling that something is wrong."

Dr. Mychael nodded. "Your gut is right. She came to me several years ago just by happenstance and has been like family to me since." She paused. "I didn't immediately know she was your daughter because she went by the name Sarah Daniels, but the more that she told me about her past, the more I realized that she was Chrystalia." She paused. "I tried to contact you to tell you, but no one that I knew before was still alive."

Ajahadé nodded. "The Chaitians have been wiped out; I'm afraid there are only a few of us left."

Dr. Mychael nodded, her face laden with sadness. "I've heard the news reports, and they haven't been good."

Ajahadé nodded again. "No, they are not good at all." She paused. "But please, tell me what you know about my baby girl."

"She has a stalker, and he has been getting closer lately, so she—" the older lady paused and got eye contact with Ajahadé. "Aj, she has vanished again. I do not know where she is."

Ajahade's face fell in deep sadness. "Do you have any idea?"

Dr. Mychael shook her head. "I wish I did, but I don't and now my grandson is gone as well."

"Who's your grandson?"

"Chase Mychael, but he also goes by CJ."

"CJ as in the pop star?"

"Yes," Dr. Mychael said, her voice showing her surprise that Ajahadé knew such a fact.

"I found out through my assistant," Ajahadé admitted. Dr. Mychael nodded and for a moment there was silence as Ajahadé processed what had just been said. Then she spoke, her voice emotionless, "Okay, I need to know everything that you know about Chrystalia, so I can figure out where she is—I'm talking about her friends, work, normal places she hangs out, and such...anything will help me at this point."

The older lady nodded her head. "Absolutely."

Location: Eastern United States

"There ya go, Chase," Brad said as he slowed the soda truck to a stop alongside the highway. "Here's where I left 'er."

Chase looked shocked. "On the side of the road in the middle of nowhere?"

"Welp, it ain't in the middle of nowhere—just looks like it. But it is definitely the side of the road." He paused as he put the truck in park. "I didn't wanna leave her here but that girl was plain insistent. I's just couldn't change 'er mind, so I did what she told me."

Chase nodded. "Thank you, Brad. I really do appreciate it." He began reaching in his pocket as though about to get money.

Brad instantly held up his hand. "Naw, don't ya give me a thing. I was a goin' this way anyway."

Chase tapped Brad on the shoulder and began climbing out of the truck. "Thank you, man."

"Yep," Brad said.

A few moments later, Chase was standing alone on the side of the road near a field. Turning, he began walking down the road and followed it as it curved to the left. Just as it curved, he spotted a gas station with a truck stop ahead.

"Howdy," the cashier said as soon as Chase walked inside the gas station. "Can I help ya?"

Chase shook his head, "I don't think so. I just want to get some refreshments."

The lady behind the counter smiled, revealing missing teeth and a crooked smile. "Ya aren't from around here, are ya?"

Chase looked perplexed. "No, but how'd you know so quickly?"

"Aw," the lady shrugged. "No one around here says 'refreshments,' nor do they have an accent like yours. Where ya from?"

"All over," he said simply. "Do you have cola?"

"Yep," she replied and pointed to a cooler in the corner. A few minutes later, he returned with a soda in his hand. "That'll be one hundred and eighty-eight pennies."

Chase looked at her in surprise for a moment and then pulled out two dollars. "Do people around here give totals in pennies?"

"Nope," the cashier said simply and then glanced back at the soda.

Chase followed her gaze and then realized that the price on the soda was only one dollar—there was no way tax was that high. "Um—" he paused.

"Yeah, you're right. The price is a dollar but some young lady told me to tell you it was 188 pennies and you'd know what it meant. I really only want one of your dollar bills, son." Perplexed, Chase gave her the dollar bill and walked out the door. He walked around to the backside of the building and sat down on the curb.

For a moment, he sat there watching as the truckers filled up their vehicles. Then he caught it—on the large yellow truck closest to him was a Pennsylvania tag with the last three digits being "188." As if on cue, he remembered Sarah's voice and giggles as she had told him one day, *"When I first came over here, I could not pronounce 'Pennsylvania' so I would call it 'the penny state.' My mom always knew what I meant."*

"188 pennies," Chase mumbled and then looked back at the tractor trailer. A short man with a bald head, glasses, and a potbelly stood outside of it pumping gas.

Chase stood up and walked over to the man. "Hello, sir," he said when he was close.

"Howdy," the truck driver responded. "Anything I can help ya with?"

"I'm not sure. I think someone told me to talk to you..." he paused, unsure how to continue.

The truck driver pushed his glasses up on his nose and tilted his head to look at Chase. "What's your name, son?"

"Chase."

"Aw." The truck driver nodded. "Yep, that lil' girl told me you'd be comin' to find me." The gas pumped clicked and the man paused to remove the nozzle from the truck. He tapped it slightly and then returned it to the pump, got his receipt, and then turned back to Chase. "She said you'd want a ride with me, so hop on in."

Chase hesitated but then got in the truck.

<><

"Alright son," the truck driver said four hours later as he pulled to the side of a narrow country road. "This is where I let her off and she told me you'd wanna be let off at the same place."

Chase nodded. "What do I owe you?"

The truck driver waved his hand. "Nothin' son, I was just comin' this way anyway."

Chase nodded and climbed out of the truck. The sun was just beginning to approach the horizon as he wandered into the woods beside the road. He walked for a little while, listening to the birds chirping from the trees. The memories of he and Sarah walking through the woods at his grandmother's place came into his mind and the longing to be with Sarah—to hear her voice and see her eyes—became so strong he could barely breathe.

He saw a pond up ahead and quickened his steps. After a few minutes, he reached the edge of the pond and sat down. For a moment, he sat there completely silent as he thought about what to do next. *Is this a dead end?*

Then he heard something stir behind him. He looked up

just in time to see a huge black and furry face lunging towards him. "Zeus!" Chase screamed just as his face became covered in slobber. He petted the big dog furiously and looked up. There, in the shadows, he saw Sarah's form slowly beginning to emerge. *She's alive.*

LOCATION: ASHEVILLE, NC

"What groceries are we getting?" Yahja asked as Ajahadé pulled the car into a parking spot at the grocery store that Dr. Mychael had told her was Chrystalia's favorite.

"Whatever you want," Ajahadé said absently.

Yahja opened her mouth to speak but stopped. Instead, she followed Ajahade's gaze and spotted two dark men sitting in a parked car several spots away.

"Are we even going to get out?"

"No," Ajahadé said, her eyes gazing the entire parking lot. *Those men—they look like Mashottiís.*

"Then what are we doing here?"

"Being quiet and watching, so please, stop talking," Ajahadé said. The younger lady finally understood and stayed quiet for several minutes.

After several long minutes, another man walked towards the parked car with the Mashottían men. Ajahadé watched as the man got into the car—without any groceries in his hand—and the car drove away.

"Are we not going to follow them?"

"No," Ajahadé said again. "There are three of them and they will catch on that they are being followed."

Yahja nodded in understanding just as Ajahadé spotted

another car nearby slowly creep forward. Looking closely, she saw that there was a man inside the car with an extended camera lens pointing toward the grocery store. She watched as the man slowly put down his camera and then began to drive away. *South Carolina license tags,* she noted.

Ajahadé turned to Yahja. "Do you have your tablet?"

"Yes."

"Okay, go to that coffee shop over there and call this person." She handed Yahja a piece of paper. "Ask about this license tag. If I do not hear from you, I'll assume you got no additional information. I'll try to be back later, but if not, just meet me at the hotel."

Yahja nodded and shifted to leave the car.

"Also," Ajahadé paused, "Please make sure you have your phone on at all times. We may need to call you in as backup."

Yahja nodded again. "Yes ma'am." With that, the younger woman left the car.

As soon as she was out, Ajahadé pulled out of the parking spot and dialed a familiar number on her phone.

"Hello?" the familiar older lady said on the other side of the phone.

"Hi," Ajahadé said in Chaitian.

"Hi Ajahadé," Dr. Mychael said in Chaitian. "What's wrong?"

"Something," Ajahadé said simply. "I'm going to the retirement home to see if I can find out anything. Meet there?"

"Sure," Dr. Mychael said and with that, the two women hung up.

A little while later, Ajahadé pulled into the parking lot of the retirement home to find Dr. Mychael standing outside. She pulled up and let Dr. Mychael climb into the car.

"Hi," Ajahadé said as soon as she was close.

"Hi," Dr. Mychael responded. "Going to see Mr. Two, I'm assuming?"

Ajahadé nodded. "And anyone who may know anything."

Dr. Mychael nodded and then got closer to Ajahadé. With her voice barely above a whisper, she spoke, "Has there been a new development?"

Ajahadé nodded. "I spotted Mashottiís here in Asheville and another person at that same store watching— perhaps her other stalker."

A look of shock and concern washed over Dr. Mychael. "Oh no, that's not good."

"Nope," Ajahadé said. "Sarah thinks she is escaping

from her father but, in truth, she is escaping from people far more dangerous."

Dr. Mychael nodded. "She's being chased by the Mashottiís. Those brutal people will stop at nothing to get what they want. She has no idea what she is up against."

Ajahadé shook her head. "And she's not equipped to deal with people in their caliber of brutality and training."

Dr. Mychael face looked gravely worried. "We've got to find her first. That's her only chance of survival."

"Sarah, I can't believe I found you," Chase said as soon as they were back to her hotel room. "I thought you would be hurt or worse when I got to you."

Sarah hugged him. "I can't believe I'm seeing you."

"Why not?"

"Because even though I knew you said you loved me, I just didn't know that you would follow my clues and come."

"Of course," he said, pulling her even closer to him. For several long moments they stayed still fully embracing each other as though afraid to let go. "I love you, Sarah." His voice was quiet.

"I love you too, Chase," she said and brought her deep brown eyes up to meet his blue ones. For a moment, time stood completely still as they stood lost in each other's gaze. Their faces drew closer.

Sarah pulled her chin up just a little to meet his. Her soft, lush lips gently brushed his. Sparks of love and attraction flew between them like fireworks on the Fourth of July. With slow and gentle movements, he reached up and brushed back the strand of hair that was falling down on her face and kissed her. His lips felt so amazing, so soft and so loving.

But then, as if on cue for breaking the moment, Sarah felt something cold poking her leg. Looking down, she saw Zeus standing below them with his ears perked up and tail wagging. "Hey boy," she said. "What's the matter? You have to go out?" He wagged his tail fiercely. "But you were just out. Are you sure?" He ran towards the door.

"I better go take him out," Sarah said. "I'm sorry."

"It's okay. I'll go with you," Chase said and followed her out of the hotel.

LOCATION: RETIREMENT HOME, USA

Ajahadé and Dr. Mychael walked down the long hallway toward Mr. Two's room, both of them hoping that he somehow had received information regarding either Sarah or Chase. However, when they knocked on the door, no one answered.

Ajahadé knocked again. "Does he usually leave and go places?"

Dr. Mychael shook her head. "No. His wife does, but he almost always stays right here or on the porch that we went by on the way in."

Ajahadé nodded and put her ear to the door. "I don't hear any movement." She paused. "I'll go get the nurse."

Dr. Mychael nodded and waited by the door. A few minutes later, Ajahadé returned with a nurse in tow.

"We haven't seen either of them today at all. We figured they were probably sleeping in or something," the nurse said and knocked on the door loudly. There was still no response. She knocked again, and yelled their names but there was still no response.

"Okay, let me get the key," she said. A few minutes later, she returned with a key and unlocked the door. She cracked it opened and yelled their names again. "Mr. Two, it's the nurse."

Still no answer so she cracked the door more. Suddenly she gasped. Instantly, Ajahadé reached for the gun hidden in her pants but stopped before exposing it. "What is it?"

"They've been hurt," the nurse said and pushed the door wide open. There, inside the Two's suite were both older people stretched out across the floor with pools of blood near each of them; the window behind them was open.

"Get back," Ajahadé said bluntly.

"I need to—"

"No," Ajahadé said firmly and the nurse obeyed. Ajahadé slowly crept inside the suite, gun in hand, and paused, listening for any sounds. Once she heard none, she slowly eased farther and farther into the suite. After several minutes of searching, she put her gun up and spoke. "It's all clear." She told the nurse, "You can go in."

The nurse nodded and a flood of nurses came up behind her. Within moments, the two older adults were whisked away on hospital beds with nurses and doctors flying alongside them shouting orders.

Ajahadé looked at Dr. Mychael. "Let's look over this place and make sure they're gone. I'll take this corridor and you take that one. Make sure you check all the closets." Dr. Mychael nodded and disappeared down the hallway.

<><

"All clear," Ajahadé said to Dr. Mychael a little while

later.

The older woman nodded. "Same here." Dr. Mychael paused, her face full of disappointment. "We missed them."

"Yep," Ajahadé said, her tone of voice emotionless, "They were stealthy. I asked all the personnel that I could and none of them saw anything out of the ordinary this morning nor did they hear from the night crew that they saw anything unusual."

Dr. Mychael nodded. "I wonder when they came."

"Not sure but it was not too long ago because they were still alive despite all the blood."

Dr. Mychael nodded. "Do you think they got any information from the Twos?"

"Probably," Ajahadé responded, her voice emotionless "The Twos probably knew that whatever information they had was a secret but probably were not aware of how important it really was…" She drifted off into thought.

"Aj," Dr. Mychael said, "are you afraid this means they're ahead of us and have already gotten Sarah?"

"Oh, they are ahead of us," Ajahadé responded frankly, "I just have to catch up." She gazed off into the distance as though constructing her next move just as a young nurse appeared in the hallway. All blood was drained from her face, her arms crossed in front of her, and her eyes were wide in fear as she slowly approached the two women.

Ajahadé looked at Dr. Mychael. Dr. Mychael looked at the young, short nurse and spoke, "Are you okay? You look scared."

The young nurse nodded and pulled her arms tighter together. Ajahadé and Dr. Mychael walked closer to her and could see her visibly shaking. "What happened?" Ajahadé asked.

"Big, tall men–" the younger lady said, her voice shaking, "th–they came and–" she paused, trying to get her breath, "they hurt the Twos and–and," she stuttered.

"Dear, are you okay? Did they hurt you?"

"I'll be okay; it hurts but not badly." Ajahadé turned and signaled to another nurse to come near.

"We're getting you help," Ajahadé said, "but did they say anything to you?"

"Yes, they were looking for Sarah–Sarah Daniels, our coordinator."

"Did they say where they were going?"

"No, but," the young nurse pulled out a piece of paper, "But the biggest one dropped this." She gave the paper to Ajahadé.

LOCATION: EASTERN UNITED STATES

Darkness filled the sky and covered the earth as Sarah slept inside the hotel room. Though normally surrounded by the sounds of the road nearby, tonight Sarah lay surrounded by a firm stillness. Silence. Nothing stirred about. At least, that's what one would think....

Then, there was a movement in the corner. Slowly, Zeus stood up and whined, waking Chase. Slowly, Chase slid out of bed and walked over to Zeus. "What is it, boy?" he whispered. The dog whined again. "Okay, I'll take you out," Chase said and grabbed for the dog's leash. Looking back, he could see that Sarah was still asleep, so he quietly walked out of the hotel room and into the night.

Chase was just out of sight when, out of quietness, a dark form moved. A dark foot gradually left the shadows. With swift movements, the man's hands flew from his side and reached for the neck of his victim....

Sarah saw him standing above her, the white of his evil eyes glaring at her through the darkness but she lay still–frozen. *This time it is not a dream,* she thought as her heart rate increased, *this is really happening.* She told her hands to move–to punch him–but they would not move. She told her voice to scream but nothing came out. It was as though her entire body rebelled against her. She was paralyzed. She could only watch in terror as the man's hands came closer and closer to her neck, his murderous intent obvious in his beady eyes.

He grabbed her neck and suddenly air vanished. She tried desperately to breathe but no air reached her lungs. The room vanished into darkness.

CHAPTER TWELVE

LOCATION: UNKNOWN

The darkness was suffocating. The room was cold. Their voices—though distant—were hushed and evil. Sarah heard footsteps approaching but could see nothing. Something was around her eyes. She tried to move her arms and legs but they were tied tightly to the chair. She heard someone breathing. *He's right at my face.*

She heard him take two steps back. Then, the man cleared his throat. When he spoke, his voice was deep and with a heavy French accent. "You—you the kid of Steliana—tell me. Where is she?"

Who is Steliana and why do they think I'm her child? Sarah thought but did not say anything. The silence, however, made the man angrier. His voice grew in volume. "Tell me! I demand you. Tell me where she is!"

"I don't know."

The man spoke again, this time between clenched

teeth. "You are trying my patience, woman. I am a patient man and the most kind of us, but you are testing me. Tell me!"

Again Sarah shook her head. "I can't tell you what I don't know."

She heard a loud stomp. "Stop treating me like a fool! I know you know who your mother is and I know you know where she is." He paused and she felt his breath on her neck. "This is the last time I ask and then you–" he paused and she felt a cold, rough finger tracing the neckline of her shirt. Instantly, the alarms going off inside grew even stronger. *He wants me sexually.* She thought, but again, stayed silent.

"You–and your beautiful body–will be longing for peace and rest as you have never known before. So," he paused, "where is Steliana!?"

Sarah stayed silent, hoping somehow to stall him. Instead, it made him angrier. He slammed his hand against her face. *Ouch!* She wanted to scream but held it in. *I can't let him know he's hurting me. Just like Richard–he can't know when he is getting close to breaking me.* He hit again. "Tell me!"

"I don't know," she said her voice still calm.

The man let out a frustrated sigh and left. A few minutes later, she heard two people approaching, their thick heavy boots pounding on the floor. She heard one of them get very close and then speak, his voice quiet and sensual, "You are so beautiful, little flower...so beautiful. Oh the things I will do to you–they will make you scream for mercy."

Sarah felt a shiver start at the top of her spine and shimmy all the way down. Fear gripped her throat. *I know exactly what is going to happen next. He is going to take my clothes off and there is literally nothing I can do to stop it. My hands and feet are bound and I have no information they want. I have no way out of this. They will rape me and then beat me until I die.* In that moment of realizing her fate, all she could see was Chase and she wanted to know that he would be okay. *My life is over now, but I want him to know that I love him.*

She felt it. The man reached for the buttons on her shirt and began slowly unbuttoning each one. "I think we both know what is going to happen next. But that is your call. You tell me what I need to know, and I will stop."

"I do not know."

"Psst! Liar!" He yanked at her shirt, and she heard the buttons fly off. *I'm without a shirt.*

"Wow," she heard another man say in the room, his voice lush with desire, "she is quite the beautiful woman." Sarah shivered again just as she felt the closest man remove her bra. *No!* She screamed inside her head, wanting just to open her eyes and find out this was all a dream, but she could not. The pain shooting from her right leg from being tied too tightly to the chair was evidence enough that this was reality.

"Yes, indeed," the first man responded and she felt his

hand go along her crotch. *Please, please don't remove my pants. Please–have mercy.* But Sarah knew there would be no such thing. "She is very beautiful. I cannot wait to–" Before the man could finish his sentence, a loud shot fired through the room. It was followed by a loud thud.

Sarah jumped. *What was that!? A gunshot? Are they killing me now?* She could hear her heartbeat pounding in her ears and could not breathe. She could not move.

Then she heard a female voice piercing through. "Get away from her!" the voice said. There was a volley of fire and thuds so loud, Sarah felt as though her eardrum exploded.

There were moans, groans, cries in pain, and then complete silence. The silence grew longer. *What just happened?* was all that Sarah could think as her heart continued to pound in her ear and her lungs struggled to breathe.

Finally, she heard someone stir and walk closer. It sounded like a lighter person than the others or someone without heavy boots. "Hi," a female voice said, "I'm going to take your blindfold off, but be prepared, there's a lot of blood. I'm here to save you."

Sarah stayed silent and then felt as rough but small hands began removing the blindfold from her eyes. Then, to her shock and amazement, she saw the very face of the woman she'd longed for since she was ten years old.

"Oh my–oh my–oh my!" Sarah stammered as tears

instantly began springing from her eyes without warning. "Mum?"

"Yes, Chrystalia, it is me," Ajahadé responded, tears flooding her own eyes. "Let me take these off your hands and feet." She pulled out a huge knife, cut away the ropes, and gave Sarah her shirt. Instantly, Sarah fell into her mother's arms.

"Oh baby, oh baby, I missed you," Ajahadé said.

Tears uncontrollably rolled down her face and nearly reached Ajahade's shoulder. Sarah responded, "I missed you too. I–I didn't think you were alive."

"I didn't think you were alive either."

Ajahadé and Sarah stayed tightly embraced for several long minutes with neither one wanting to move. It was like they were afraid that if they let go, they would somehow lose each other. Finally after a long time, Sarah slowly pulled back and looked at her mother's now-aged faced. It was scarred in many places, especially around her neck. "Wh–what happened to you, Mum?"

"What do you mean?"

"Your face–it has more scars."

"Oh, yes," Ajahadé said, waving her hand, "just battle scars."

"What happened to Daddy and everyone?"

Ajahadé slowly shook her head in sadness. "It's only us."

Sarah nodded, biting her lower lip. "I was afraid you'd say that."

Ajahadé nodded. "Yes." She slowly pulled back. It was then that Sarah got a glimpse of what was in the room. There were eight huge men—muscular and military built—lying crumbled and bloody on the floor. There were pools of blood on the floor surrounding the dead bodies.

"Whoa," was all Sarah could muster as the reality of the situation began to appear. She put her arms into her shirt and pulled it closed since it no longer had buttons. "You did this alone?"

Ajahadé followed her gaze to the dead bodies and then looked back up at her daughter, nodded, and then spoke. "No one—" she paused and then continued her voice strong, "I repeat—*no one* kidnaps, then tries to rape and kill my daughter without answering to me."

<><

"Where are we going?" Sarah asked as Ajahadé led her through the abandoned warehouse where she had been held hostage. "Where's Chase?"

"He got kidnapped as well but my assistant and the doc got him. They are supposed to meet us at our spot," Ajahadé said as she climbed on top of a plank in the floor. "Watch your step. The floor has rotted out so you have to walk on this plank." Sarah nodded and followed.

"Do you think that was all of the bad guys?"

"No, there are more, but they aren't going to dare come close now." Ajahadé paused. "But we'll talk about it later, not here—okay?" Sarah nodded and followed her mother to the car.

Sarah got on the passenger side and sat down. *Wow, this seat feels so soft.* Ajahadé sat down in the driver seat and started the car. "How long has it been since you've driven?" Sarah asked.

"Up until this trip..." Ajahadé paused. "Wow, it's been years. Probably over twelve years."

"I bet it felt weird coming back to it."

"It did but I had some practice before I left."

"People have cars in Chaiti now?"

"No, it is still a lot the way it was when you were there— probably worse actually—because the war has made people very, very poor. Almost no one has cars. They just walk everywhere."

"Makes sense," Sarah responded and watched out the window as Ajahadé took several turns.

"Are you not afraid we'll be followed?"

Ajahadé shook her head. "No, I was followed there and I killed everyone. They don't have any more backups here."

Unsure how to respond, Sarah stayed quiet until they pulled into a hotel parking lot. A few minutes later, they were upstairs and Ajahadé was opening the door to a room. "Go on in," she said and waited until Sarah entered.

Inside sat a young Chaitian woman and beside her stood the man of her dreams. Without hesitation, she ran into his arms. "Oh, Chase! You are safe!"

He grabbed her, picked her up into his arms, and spun her around the room. "Yes! And so are you!" She laughed. "I was so worried," he said.

He slowly put her down but continued to hold her close. She could feel his heart beating. The moments stretched on.

That's when she heard Ajahade's speak quietly, "Yahja, let's give them some time." She paused. "Chrystalia, we'll be down in the lobby eating if you need anything." Sarah nodded her acknowledgement but didn't stray from Chase's embrace.

After several long moments, she looked up. She could see Dr. Mychael standing next to them with tears trickling down her wrinkled face.

"Sarah, my dear," she paused, overwhelmed with emotions, "you are alive. We feared the worse."

Sarah stretched out her hand and pulled Dr. Mychael into their hug. "I can't say how happy I am to see you."

"Me too." Chase and Dr. Mychael said at the same time. For several long minutes the three of them embraced before finally, Sarah pulled back. She turned to Chase and spoke with tears in her eyes, "I'm so glad you are okay–I thought they had killed you."

"Me too." He responded and hugged her again. "I was so afraid you were gone."

After a long while, she pulled back from him slightly and then looked up into his beautiful blue eyes. "I love you, Chase."

"I love you too, Sarah."

LOCATION: HOTEL LOBBY HALF-HOUR LATER

"Hi, honey," Ajahadé said as Sarah and Chase—hand in hand—approached the table where Ajahadé and Yahja sat talking by a fireplace. Dr. Mychael was close behind them.

"Hi, Mum." Sarah paused. "Have you officially met Chase?"

Ajahadé looked hesitant. "No, not officially, but it's great to meet you," she replied and looked up into his eyes. "Are you Sarah's boyfriend?"

Without hesitation, Chase nodded as he pulled out a chair for Sarah to sit down. "I am." He then sat down next to Sarah and held her hand.

"That's great. I'm glad to hear my girl has someone. How long have you guys known each other?"

Sarah and Chase both hesitated. Sarah finally spoke, "A long time. We met while I was still with my adoptive parents. We were just teenagers at the time. Then things happened with our families and we broke contact. We finally found each other a few months ago."

Ajahadé looked intrigued but hesitated to ask more questions. "I'll ask more questions later," she said, "but first, let's grab some food from here and go back to the room so we can talk." Everyone nodded.

A little while later they were back in the hotel room and sitting comfortably. "So," Sarah asked, "what is all this about? Who were those men?"

"Mashottiís," Ajahadé said frankly as though it explained everything.

"Who are the Mashottiís?" Chase asked timidly.

"The enemy of Chaitians."

"Oh," Chase said. "I saw on TV that there was a civil war going on..." He let the sentence hang.

"Yes," Ajahadé stood up and walked over to the window. After a few moments, she turned back, her face emotionless. "Chaiti used to be a democracy—kind of like the United States—and, in fact, were quite friendly with the US. Our ruler—well, more like a prime minister—was called Chief Sengj, and he lived in our version of the White House, except we called it the Palace."

Sarah opened her mouth to speak so Ajahadé paused. "Yes Sarah?"

"The Palace—as in your work place where we used to get the horses?"

"Yes," Ajahadé nodded. "I worked in the Palace with Chief Sengj."

"And you used to go in and out freely with Sarah?" Chase asked.

Again, Ajahadé nodded. "Yes, but just with her because, Chrystalia—or Sarah—is my adopted daughter."

Sarah's face dropped in shock. For a long time, there was complete silence as she processed what had just been said. Finally she spoke, her voice timid, "If you aren't my biological mother, then who is?"

"Steliana."

"Steliana?" Sarah asked, her voice inundated with shock. "That's the name those men kept asking me about—it's like they somehow knew she was my biological mother."

"They did, and I knew you didn't know. I tried so hard to find you before they did." Sarah looked confused so Ajahadé continued, "Your mother was Chief Sengj's daughter. She was a wild child and very hard to pin down—always pushing the rules and escaping off to places. Then one day she came back pregnant. She didn't tell me who the father was but she knew she could not take care of the baby—she was still a child herself, just a teenager. I was pregnant at the time with my second child so we came up with a plan. She hid her pregnancy from the people and even from her father and then, when I gave birth, we said that I had twins." She paused. "Everyone believed us."

"So Jajge was not my biological twin brother?"

Ajahadé shook her head. "No, but he was still your brother. You were our child." Sarah nodded and Ajahadé continued, "I took you to the Palace on occasion so Steliana could see you. Eventually, Chief Sengj found out as well, so he got to see you, too."

Sarah felt Chase gently squeeze her hand; he put one arm over her shoulder and pulled her closer.

"Anyway, back when we were in power—we, as in the Chaitians—our government was strong and our people were happy. We had freedoms but then—" she paused as though retrieving a memory she had wanted to forget, "then one day everything changed."

There were several moments of silence as she looked off into the window as though gathering her thoughts. She then turned back and looked Sarah in the eyes. "Then everything changed. Somehow the Mashottiís found out a lot about us and they overthrew the government from the inside out. They captured my family and held them hostage. Eventually they got me as well and things got awful..." She paused as the memories came flooding back. "I thought you'd died, too."

"You left me in our secret spot in the woods," Sarah said, the memories coming back to her as well.

"Yes, I did and one of my associates was supposed to get you to safety, but I later found her dead."

"She did, Mum," Sarah said.

Ajahadé turned and looked at Sarah. "How?"

"She came to me when I was in our spot and told me to follow her but to be very, very quiet; so I did. She took me to this house where an American missionary couple lived, and she left me there. I don't know what happened to her after that."

"She must have been captured after that then..." Ajahade's voice trailed off. "And then what happened?"

"The American took me to this place—I forget what it is called—but it was an organization of some sort, and that organization took me to the US where I was in foster care for a little while then placed with my adoptive parents."

Ajahadé looked thoughtful. "That must be why I could not find you..." her voice trailed off. "The American organization was not part of our plan." Ajahadé looked back at Sarah, "How were your adopted parents? Did they love you?"

"The father was abusive," Dr. Mychael said quietly, barely above a whisper.

A look of anger and rage flashed over Ajahade's face. "What did he do to you, my baby girl?"

Sarah looked out the window and off into the distance as she tried to push down the feelings that were threatening to appear at the thought of Richard and the past. "He hurt me in many ways, Mum."

Ajahade's face grew in controlled anger. "Did he manipulate you? Beat you? Sexually abuse you?"

"Yes," Sarah said simply.

"Yes to which?"

"All," Sarah said her voice low and timid.

Ajahadé looked angry but said nothing for several moments. Finally, she spoke, "What was his name?"

"Richard Daniels."

"Where does he live?"

"He used to live outside Summerville, South Carolina."

"What'd he do for a living?"

"Plummer."

"Wife?"

"Charleen Daniels."

"Okay." Ajahadé paused and then continued, her voice low. "You won't have to worry about him anymore."

A confused looked flashed on all their faces but faded from Sarah's face the fastest as she recalled her mother's words in the warehouse. *"No one kidnaps, then attempts to rape and kill my daughter without answering to me."* Though Sarah suspected Ajahadé meant she was personally going to get justice served to Richard, Sarah decided not to clarify. *Some things I don't want to know.*

"But I am worried," Sarah said.

"Why, honey?" Dr. Mychael asked.

"I sent my adopted mother a message that should have

helped her to find me, but she never showed."

"When was the last time you heard from her?"

"Years ago," Sarah said. "Even though I think some part of her loved me, she wasn't strong enough to stand up for or defend me; so it was too dangerous to tell her where I was..." Sarah's voice trailed off.

"Then why did you send her the message?"

"Because I have a feeling that she was in trouble, and I was hoping she would come to me, so I could help her get away from him."

Ajahadé nodded. "Well, I will try to find her–okay?"

Sarah nodded. After a few moments of silence, she spoke, "So what happened to my biological mother?"

"She vanished but we later found out that she was the one who had enabled the Mashottiís to overtake our government," Ajahadé responded, her voice matter-of-fact.

"Why?" Sarah and Chase said at the same time.

Ajahadé shook her head. "I don't know. I suspect she may have been romantically involved with the leader of the Mashottiís–people call him Prince Randhiji–and that caused her to do what she did, but I'm not sure. I cannot conceive it."

Everyone in the room shook their heads. "Wait–if she is the one who provided information or whatever that got them to take over, then why were they looking for her?" Chase asked.

"Because she got cold feet and vanished instead of staying with them. No one knew where she was—not even they knew."

"You used past tense," Sarah said, "Does that mean her location is now known?"

Ajahadé looked serious. "Perhaps. But we'll have to see. The important thing now is that they know for sure that you don't know and they are not going to come for you anymore."

"You think they realized that?" Sarah asked in surprise.

"Yes, they did. I could tell by the way they were acting they knew you were being honest. I also allowed one of them time to send that message to their leader—who is back in Chaiti—before I killed them. So you should not be chased anymore."

A feeling of relief and comfort swept over Sarah at the sound of those words. Part of her wanted to believe them but the other part—the part that had been on edge and constantly watching over her shoulder for the last decade—was hesitant to believe such a truth existed. Chase pulled her closer. She slid even closer into his arms.

"That's great news," Chase said to Ajahadé.

"Yes, indeed it is," Ajahadé said.

CHAPTER THIRTEEN

LOCATION: ASHEVILLE, NC
TIME: TWO DAYS LATER

Sarah and Chase walked down the off-white hallway and towards the familiar room within the retirement home. Just as they approached, a nurse walked out. "Oh! Hi, Sarah, so glad to see you're okay."

Sarah smiled. "Thanks," she paused, "how are they?"

"They are good. They lost a lot of blood—mostly because of their blood thinners—but they are recovering well after the transfusions that the hospital gave them. So, I think they are going to be just fine."

Sarah let out a breath of relief. "I'm so glad."

The nurse tapped Sarah on the shoulder. "Me too," she said and walked away.

Chase knocked on the door and waited until Mr. Two responded before entering. Mr. and Mrs. Two were sitting in their recliners watching TV. They looked up to see Sarah and Chase.

"Oh, my goodness! Ya'll are all right!" Mr.Two said, "We were so worried about ya!"

Sarah smiled. "Yes, we are okay but we heard you two had a hard time."

"Why yes, we did," he said seriously, "but we'll be alright."

"We're tough," Mrs. Two said and then sipped her tea. "This one here—" she pointed to her husband, "survived two wars. I survived two bouts of cancer, a major car accident, and a fire. So, we're tough." Sarah smiled.

"I'm glad. We were so worried."

"Aw, dear, that's so nice of ya. But we're fine. How are you? Come tell me about what happened." Mr. Two said and pointed to the couch. "Move them pillows if ya want."

Sarah and Chase sat down and began telling them the story. Once they were finished, Mr. and Mrs. Two's chins dropped. "Wow," Mr. Two said, "I had no idea you were a fugitive, my dear. You're quite a tough one too."

Sarah looked thoughtful, "I guess you're right, Mr. Two. Guess I am kinda tough."

"Yes, you sure are, dear," Mrs. Two responded.

LOCATION: RICHARD DANIEL'S HOUSE
TIME: THREE DAYS LATER

It was a rainy and dreary night as Richard angrily walked up the stairs to his house. He fumbled with his keys, dropping them on the concrete twice before finally getting one of them into the keyhole and turning it.

His annoyance growing, he entered the dark living room and shut the door. He turned on the lamp and saw his beaten wife still lying on the living room floor—just as he'd left her.

"Ya worthless piece of crap. Ya warned her I was goin' for her! It is your fault that I couldn't find her!" he screamed, as he stormed over and kicked her with his heavy boots. However, his foot suddenly got trapped in her hands; his foot twisted then flew out from underneath him. He landed on the wood floor with a thud, face first, and felt a strong foot on his neck. That's when he realized the woman on the floor was not his wife.

"'Worthless piece of crap,'" a strong and angered woman's voice said in a heavy accent. "Is that what you call the love of your life and the woman who raised your daughter?"

"It's exactly what she is," he responded. Ajahadé jabbed her foot into his neck even harder.

"Is that what you called your daughter too?"

"Yup, that's what she is! That worthless thing."

"No!" Ajahadé responded and kicked him. "They are not worthless and they did not deserve what you did to them. *You* are the worthless piece of crap and *you* deserve to be tortured and killed for what you did."

He scoffed at her from his position beneath her on the floor. "Yeah, like ya could do that."

"You bet I could," she responded. "I was trained in military torture techniques; I have killed more people than you can count. It was part of my job, and I have no problem doing it again." She paused. "Torture is exactly what you deserve. You deserve to feel pain so strong that you beg to be killed because then you will understand that there are things worse than death."

Richard swallowed hard.

"But even that will not be enough. You have hurt your wife and daughter beyond words. No physical pain will come close to the damage you did to them."

She felt him breathe a little beneath her grip. "So ya gonna let me go?"

"Oh no," she said. "I am going to kill you." She paused and he could feel the cold gun on the back of his head. "But I first want you to know that your wife is nearly dead because of you. And *you* are a worthless piece of crap. The gods will show you no mercy. After you die, you will get the torture you deserve–for eternity."

Then, without hesitation, she pulled the trigger.

LOCATION: THE MYCHAEL ESTATE
TIME: FOUR DAYS AFTER RESCUE

The sun was shining between the clouds as Sarah and Chase sat on the bench in the backyard. Several birds were chirping in the distance and Zeus was stretched out on the cool stone porch. Sarah sat quietly watching as the water in the fountain rose and fell.

"Are you okay?" Chase asked as put his arm around her shoulders and pulled her closer.

"I think so, it just has been a lot to process."

"I can imagine." He put his free hand on her knee and she grabbed his hand. Holding her hand, he continued, "Do you want to talk about it?"

"It's just hard to believe that my mom was not my biological mother, that my brother and sister and dad are dead, and that my grandfather is Chief Sengj." She paused. "And I do not know what Mum is doing to Richard. I can only imagine."

"Do you think she got to Mrs. Daniels before it was too late?"

Sarah shook her head. "I don't know," she bit her bottom lip, "but I have a bad feeling."

About that time, Zeus jerked his head up and looked towards the house. Sarah turned and followed his gaze. Standing near the doorway on the porch was Ajahadé with Dr. Mychael close behind.

"Mum," Sarah said and stood up. Chase followed her, and they walked over to Ajahadé. "Are you okay?"

"Yes," Ajahadé said quietly but her face expression was serious. Sensing they needed to be alone, Dr. Mychael and Chase excused themselves and went inside.

Once alone, Sarah looked at her mother. With concern in her eyes, she asked, "Mum, what's wrong?"

Ajahade's face was solemn and her gaze low as she spoke, "Chrystalia, my dear, I saw your mum."

"And?" Sarah bit her lip, "is she okay?"

Ajahadé shook her head. "No, she is in really bad shape but I got her to the hospital and she is getting the care she needs."

Sarah felt tears beginning to accumulate behind her eyes. "Wh-what happened?" she stuttered.

Ajahadé bit her lower lip to hold back her emotions, "Do you really want to know?" Sarah nodded. "She—" Ajahadé paused as though struggling to find the words.

"Just tell me straight."

Ajahadé nodded slowly. "It looks as though Richard beat her nearly to death."

Without warning, the floodgate broke and Sarah burst into tears. Ajahadé held her close and rubbed her back until the tears subsided.

Finally, Sarah spoke, her voice hoarse, "Thanks for telling me."

Ajahadé nodded as she brushed away a clump of wet hair from Sarah's face. "Chrystalia," she paused, "the story is not finished. I got there too late to defend her because Richard had already done it, but I still got there before he returned."

Sarah's eyes widened with interest. "And you saw him?"

"Yes, I saw him. And he's taken care of now. You no longer have to be concerned with him."

Sarah looked hesitant. "If he's in jail, he's been there before and has connections..." Her voice trailed off just as she looked at Ajahadé.

"No, he is not in jail nor is he free, Chrystalia." She paused. "Richard Daniels is dead."

Suddenly, a whirlwind of emotions flew through Sarah. A mix of emotions so strong and yet hard to understand. She felt relieved and yet guilty for feeling relieved; surprised he was dead but not shocked given how Ajahadé had fought the Mashottiís; she felt pain and worry for Mrs. Daniels followed by more relief that she was found in time to get care. The emotions became so strong and so hard to understand that she simply began to cry.

Ajahadé pulled Sarah close again. "Chrystalia, my baby girl, I love you. You are safe from him now and you are not alone."

Slowly, her words began to resonate with Sarah and the grief turned to relief. *I am safe now. No more running, no more hiding, no more second-guessing everyone I know. It is over. I am safe.*

Just as the thoughts began to settle in, she heard footsteps approaching and looked up to see Dr. Mychael and Chase returning. Their faces were solemn and heavy with concern. "Sarah," Chase said as soon as he was within hearing distance, "I just heard. I'm so sorry about your mother."

Sarah walked to him and fell into his arms. He stroked her hair for several long minutes as she cried. After a little while, she pulled back and looked over at Ajahadé. "Where is she? Which hospital?"

"I'll show you," Ajahadé responded.

<><

The lighting was bright, the walls were plain white, and the temperature was cold as Sarah and Ajahadé walked down the long hospital hallway. Dr. Mychael and Chase had come as well but had to remain in the waiting room as only two people were allowed in Mrs. Daniels' room at a time.

A nurse was exiting the room as they approached. "How is she?" Sarah asked.

"We just checked her vitals. The doctor will be here in about ten minutes and will give you an update." Sarah nodded and walked into the room.

On the bed was the pale, deathly thin woman who looked only like the shell of the woman she remembered. There were many tubes and machines were making clicking noises. Her eyes were closed.

Sarah approached the bed quietly and, for a moment, just watched Mrs. Daniels. "Mom," Sarah said quietly, "it's me–Sarah."

Instantly, her eyes opened. Her blue eyes looked at Sarah's face thoroughly, as though she could not believe them. Then, as the realization that it was reality occurred, tears began streaming down the pale woman's face.

"Sarah, my baby, you're here. You're alive."

Tears swelled up in Sarah's eyes. "Yes, I'm here."

Just as the tears came trickling down Mrs. Daniel's face, a look of panic swept in. "Sarah, you can't stay here–he is coming back. He's angry."

"No, Mom," Sarah said calmly. "It is okay. He is not a worry anymore."

Mrs. Daniels looked confused. Sarah stepped back and motioned for Ajahadé to come forward. "Mom, this is my mother from Chaiti who the missionaries thought had died."

Mrs. Daniels looked surprised, but smiled. Sarah said, "She's the one who saved you. She defended you from Richard and made you safe now."

It took several minutes for Mrs. Daniels to process that information. "You turned him in?"

Ajahadé shook her head. "No, but I took care of him. He is no longer able to hurt you or Sarah or anyone. He's dead."

"You killed him?" Mrs. Daniels looked fearful and surprised.

"Yes, after getting clearance to do so from my government."

Mrs. Daniels still looked confused. "I don't understand. Why would your government care about us?"

Ajahade's face changed to expressionless, as though she was flipping into her professional persona. "Because of who Sarah is by birth. She is the birth granddaughter of someone very important within our government, and our government has been trying to find her since she disappeared during the war. When we found her and determined she was in danger, we eliminated the threat."

Mrs. Daniels nodded her understanding just as the doctor appeared in the room. He was a short man, with dark rimmed glasses. After checking her vitals again, he spoke, "You've been through a lot," he paused and pushed up his glasses, "but it looks like you are going to be okay. Going to need to stay here for a few more days and you'll need some physical therapy, but I expect a full recovery."

Sarah and Ajahadé both sighed in relief.

The doctor looked over at them. "Yes, it looks like whoever saved her got there just in time. Much longer and I'm afraid I wouldn't have this good news." Ajahadé nodded and the doctor left the room.

The moment the door shut, Mrs. Daniels looked at Ajahadé and spoke, her voice soft, "Thank you. Thank you so much for saving me."

Ajahadé nodded. "I'm just glad that I made it in time."

Mrs. Daniels nodded. "Me too."

"Sarah?" Mrs. Daniels said after a few moments. Sarah came closer to the bed. "Thank you for coming back for me."

"Of course, Mom. It killed me not knowing how you were, but I knew if I signaled to you, he'd find out, and it'd make things worse."

"But you did, dear. I got your message."

"You did?"

"Yes, and I was trying to come but the signal was so convoluted that I couldn't figure it out in time before he came back and—" she paused, "well, you know what happened."

"So my signal got you here?" Sarah asked, her heart hitting the floor.

"No, no dear," Mrs. Daniels said, "None of this is your fault. Richard did what he did because of who he is and not because of anyone else." Sarah nodded but the tears still pooled in her eyes. "Oh honey," Mrs. Daniels said, "Please don't take any of this as yours. You and Ajahadé saved me." She reached out her hands and pulled Sarah close. "I will never be able to thank you enough."

LOCATION: MYCHAEL ESTATE
TIME: FOUR DAYS LATER

The light was dim in Dr. Mychael's library as Sarah sat in the leather chair, soaking up the fading sunlight. She heard footsteps approaching and looked up to see Ajahadé approaching. "Hi, Mum," she whispered.

"Hey," Ajahadé responded and sat down next to her. For a moment they both sat in silence. "I heard from your grandfather."

"Chief Sengj?"

Ajahadé nodded. "He cannot wait to see you."

Sarah smiled. "I can't wait to see him either. It has been so long–I'm afraid I won't remember him."

"You will," Ajahadé responded. "He's hard to forget."

Sarah nodded. "How long have you worked for him?"

"Hm," Ajahadé paused, "since I was really young."

"How old?"

"I don't know - no one knows my birth date. We don't keep records like that. I'd guess that I was under ten years old though."

"Wow," Sarah said, "that's incredible." Ajahadé simply nodded. "How long is he going to let you stay here?"

"Not much longer. I will be leaving at dawn."

Sarah's face flashed sadness. "But I have just begun to get to know you again. It hasn't been long enough, Mum. We've got so much more to talk about."

"I know, dear," Ajahadé responded, her voice echoing Sarah's sadness. "But I have some things I need to take care of back home. There's a war going on, and my brother is missing."

Sarah nodded, remembering an earlier conversation on the topic. "I know, but please promise me you'll be back."

"I will, and I want to take you to see Chief Sengj."

"In Chaiti?"

"No, he isn't in Chaiti. He's at another location."

Sarah opened her mouth to ask where but saw the look on Ajahade's face and knew she would not say.

"Okay," Sarah said. "I'll go, as long as I'm with you."

"Absolutely." Ajahadé paused. "You get Mrs. Daniels settled in here with Dr. Mychael so that she can recover—both physically and emotionally. She's got a long way to go but I am fully confident that Dr. Mychael will help her to recover. And then I'll come back for you."

Sarah looked sad but nodded her agreement, "Okay. Is there a way I can contact you?"

"Not directly. I will be working so I'll go dark for a while but," she paused, "if you are ever in danger, Dr. Mychael will know the signals to get me to return."

A look of curiosity flashed over Sarah's face but she did not ask any questions. Instead, she nodded. "Mum," she paused.

"Yes?"

"I love you. Please stay safe. I can't bear the thought of losing you again."

Ajahadé bit her lip to hold back tears. "I love you too, and I will. I won't stay away very long." And, with that, Ajahadé stood up, hugged her, and then vanished into the darkness.

The sun was shining brightly through the office window as Chief Sengj spoke, "That is a job well done," he said to Ajahadé as she sat across from his desk inside his familiar office. "Our girl is safe."

Ajahadé nodded. "I will bring her to visit you as soon as I can make arrangements."

The older man nodded. "Yes, I was informed of that. I am anxious to see her and her boyfriend."

Ajahadé nodded. "As are they to see you."

A small smile stretched across the diplomat's wrinkled face as he stood next to the window. There were a few moments of silence before he responded. "The war has slowed, but we still need a strategy. Were you able to find out anything about Steliana?"

"I found her," Ajahadé said simply.

"Does she know you found her?"

"Not yet," Ajahadé said, "but since they are looking for her, if we are able to get to her first, we may be able to get her to help us."

"Perhaps." He looked hesitant. "They may trust her, and she could be our eyes and ears, but—" he paused, "that's assuming she is remorseful and is trustworthy enough."

"We'll keep her on a short leash," Ajahadé said emotionlessly.

The diplomat nodded. "Does this mean you're back on the job?"

Ajahadé paused for a moment. "Yes sir."

Chief Sengj said nothing but the small smile on his lips was enough to show his satisfaction. "Well," he said frankly, "then I best let you say hello to your help." With that, he opened the door and then—one by one—each member of Ishnomela's family came into the dimly lit office.

"Oh my! You are alive!" Ajahadé screamed as she hugged each of her nephews, sister-in-law, and her brother. "Ish, I was so worried."

He hugged her back. "I'm glad you are okay. We saw your hut—it is demolished."

Ajahadé nodded and turned her attention to the pale, thin woman standing behind her brother. "Jarah," she said simply and walked over to her.

The pale woman reached out and embraced Ajahadé with firmness. "Thank you," she said between tears, "for saving me." Ajahadé hugged her tighter.

"Of course," Ajahadé responded and then she caught Ishnomela looking at her, his face giving her the signal that he had more to say.

After a few minutes, Chief Sengj dismissed everyone

except Ishnomela and Ajahadé. Once the door was closed, he turned to face both of them. "We've got a lot of work to do."

They both nodded, but Ajahade's face showed she was not happy. "What is it that bothers you, Ajahadé?" Chief Sengj asked.

She paused a moment before responding, "What happened? Were we right that Ish's hut was set up to look as though he had been kidnapped?"

Chief Sengj paced in front of the window for a moment before looking at Ishnomela. "Ishnomela, you take this one."

"Yes sir," he responded and then turned to Ajahadé, "Yes. You are correct. I staged it to look like the Mashottiís had taken us so that you would join the action."

Ajahade's face turned red in anger but she said nothing. The moments stretched on. She could hear the clock above Chief Sengj ticking. "Why? Why did you do that?"

"I was desperate."

Ajahade's eyes darted back and forth as she tried to contain her anger, "You—you made me think that you were dead. That your wife and children were kidnapped, tortured, or killed! You made me worry that you were being tortured. All of this so that I would do something against my own will!? On top of that, do you realize that people died because of that? Bahja, the man who vowed to be there for me if I ever needed to escape, was tortured and killed because he helped me to escape—escape so that I could find you!"

Ishnomela's face was pale and his eyes showed his sadness and pain. "You're right." He said simply, "I did. And I did it out of desperation."

For several more minutes, there was silence. Finally, Ajahadé spoke, her voice nearly expressionless, "How can I trust you after this?"

Ishnomela stayed quiet, unable to answer. That's when Chief Sengj spoke, his deep voice serious and focused, "You can trust that he will do the best for his country, even if it means potentially sacrificing a few individuals to save the masses. In this case, he sacrificed Bahja to save many others and to set us up to save more. While I do not agree with his methods or tactics, I can see that his motivation was solid."

Ajahadé looked thoughtful as she processed that information. Chief Senjg had a point. Ishnomela's decision, though questionable, had helped to save Chrystalia, Mrs. Daniels, all of Ishnomela's family, Jarah, and had positioned them to contact Steliana. Not to mentioned, Ajahadé had killed many elite Mashottiian fighters in the process. This, no doubt, would lead to an advantage in the war.

Chief Sengj spoke again, this time looking at Ishonomela, "But from now on, Ajahadé and I will call the shots." Ishonomela nodded. "Now, let's get started on our strategy." Both siblings nodded.

CHAPTER FOURTEEN

LOCATION: NORTH CAROLINA COAST
TIME: THREE WEEKS LATER

The sun was shining brightly against the cloudless sky as Sarah, dressed in a beautiful purple dress with high heel shoes, walked down the stone steps of Chase's vacation house and toward the black sedan sitting in the driveway. Expecting to see the driver standing next to the car, she was surprised to see Chase standing there, his eyes on her.

"Wow, you look amazing," he said, his voice soft, "Just wow."

She smiled and felt her face warm as she looked at his black suit and blue shirt. "You look sharp yourself."

He pulled her close and kissed her gently. "I'm so glad we are able to do this."

"Me too," she replied quietly and then stepped back so he could help her into the vehicle. He closed her door and then walked around to the other side and got in beside her in the back seat. Once they were settled, the driver started the car and began driving towards their destination.

"I've wanted to take you to this place for so long but we just couldn't," Chase said.

Sarah nodded. "I'm so glad we get do to things now, without fear."

"Well, we may still have to worry about paparazzi but nothing else, and I've tried to keep those down."

A few minutes later, the driver pulled the vehicle into the parking lot of the restaurant and dropped them off at the front door. Going inside, Sarah watched as the restaurant staff led them through the restaurant and to a private dining section that overlooked the Intercoastal Waterway.

"Does this work?" the hostess asked.

Chase nodded. "This is nice, thank you." The hostess nodded and disappeared.

Once they were seated, Sarah looked at the view and watched as seagulls flew over the water. "This is beautiful."

"I'm glad. I know how much you like seafood given that you grew up on the island, and I thought this would be a good way to give you a taste of home."

"That's so nice of you," Sarah responded. *But the American seafood is not seasoned the same way as Chaitian food, so it is very different...*she thought.

"The chef here," Chase paused, "is from Chaiti

originally, and he tries to incorporate a lot of the island flavors into the food. People say it is very good."

Sarah's mouth opened in shock. "Really? I had no idea North Carolina had something like this."

"They don't," he responded, a teasing grin around his lips. "I arranged for this chef to come here tonight. The restaurant owner is a friend and allowed it."

"Seriously?"

"Yes, I wanted tonight to be special. It's your birthday!"

Sarah felt her eyes beginning to get teary as she reached across the table and grabbed his hand. "That is so nice of you, Chase." He smiled just as the waitress appeared to take their order.

"So, Chase," Sarah began after they had placed their order, "what are your plans after this?"

"Well, after this we are going to go on a boat ride..." He paused.

"Oh, that's great!" Sarah said, "I'm excited now although I actually meant your plans in general. Like if you are going to be leaving and traveling again."

"I will eventually, yes. I have to get back on tour, but I am waiting until you're settled better and the lawsuit dies down a little bit."

"What do you mean, 'I'm settled better'? You don't have to wait for me."

He paused and drew his beautiful blue eyes up to meet hers. "Sarah, I love you, and it killed me when I lost you before. I knew you relatively well then, but I know you even better now. Honestly, I can't imagine living without you." He paused. "I couldn't get myself to leave you."

Sarah swallowed hard. "I love you too, Chase. I know what life without you is like, and I want you in my life. You're my best friend, and I want to go on adventures with you."

"Would you come with me on tour?"

Sarah thought hard for several minutes. "Yes, I would. But I need some time to heal first. It is tough," she said. "I want to be with you and, even though I know Richard is not here anymore, there is still a part of me that is scared of being exposed and out in the open. It goes against everything I've ever known."

"Did you like being in the shadows and running?" Chase's voice was thoughtful.

"No, I didn't. In fact, every day I longed for stability and safety."

"Do you feel safe now?"

"Not yet. I feel safer but not completely safe. I don't think it has completely hit me yet."

"And that's what I meant," he said gently. "Once you feel safe you'll feel more settled and able to decide when you want to come with me. But right now it's tough to think like that because you are so used to surviving by being in the shadows."

"But I want to be with you. I want to go with you. I just need time to process all this."

"Okay," he said gently, "I will just take my time and we'll get back out there when you are ready. I have time. I need to concentrate on this lawsuit and it will take a while before it is settled."

"Are you sure you want to put your career on hold for me?"

"Absolutely," he squeezed her hand, "I love you over my career. I also know what it is like to be in the spotlight. I don't know what it is like to hide in the shadows, but I know what the spotlight is like and it's harsh in its own right. I want to make sure you are as ready for it as you can be before we go back."

"Thank you, Chase," she said quietly.

"You're welcome, babe." He paused. "Plus, we need to practice together and you need to write more songs."

"You want me to play the piano and write for you?" Sarah looked surprised.

"Yes! I sure do."

"What about your pianist?"

"He'll be my backup in case you get the flu or something."

Sarah smiled just as the waitress brought their food. A few moments later, she took her first bite. "Oh my goodness, this is delicious!"

Chase smiled. "I'm so glad."

"Yes! This is amazing. It really reminds me a lot of the fish that Mum and I used to eat in the Palace. It was seasoned just like this."

Chase smiled. "I'm so glad."

<><

The light was beginning to fade as Chase and Sarah walked towards the canoe that was sitting in the water by the pier, "Chase, I just don't know if this is going to work..." Sarah said. "I'm wearing a dress."

"True..." Chase's voice trailed off. "And I'm wearing a suit."

"Yeah, but I'll give it a try if you want."

Chase shrugged. "People do it overseas all the time at the river walks and such..."

"Okay, I'll try. Worse case, I'll just get my dress wet."

Chase smiled and pulled the canoe closer to the pier. "I'll get in first so I can help stabilize it and then I'll help you in. Okay?"

"Sure," Sarah responded and watched as he put one foot into the boat. Suddenly he lost his balance, the boat rocked, and he fell straight into the water. "Chase!" Sarah yelled.

His head popped up a few feet away. "I'm okay, I'm okay," he said and swam to the pier. He grabbed the side of the pier and pulled himself up.

"Oh my goodness, Chase!" Sarah said, hardly able to hold back the giggles.

Chase laughed. "Man! I can't mount a horse, and

apparently I can't get into a canoe either!"

Sarah laughed. "I guess not!" She shook her head. "Are you okay?"

"Yes," he said, still laughing, "just embarrassed. I was trying so hard to be smooth and failed."

Sarah laughed. "Well, it's okay. At least you're okay."

Chase nodded. "Would you be okay if we go back to the house so I can change?"

"Sure," Sarah responded.

<><

"This was a wonderful date, Chase," Sarah said as they walked along the pier about an hour later.

"Really? I was afraid the mishap with the boat would make it the worse date ever."

"Oh no," Sarah waved her hand, "that made it even more awesome. I don't think I've seen your face turn that red before."

He laughed. "I'm not ever going to live that down, am I?"

"Nope," Sarah said matter-of-factly.

Chase laughed just as they reached the end of the pier. Pulling her close and wrapping his arms around her waist, they faced the water and watched as the sun approached the horizon. Several seagulls flew along the water, calling out their familiar songs. "This is such a beautiful sunset."

"Sure is," Chase responded, "with a beautiful lady."

Sarah smiled and turned around to face him, "Thanks, babe."

The wind blew her hair away from her face as she brought her deep brown eyes to meet his. He pulled her even closer to him and spoke, his voice was soft, "I love you, Sarah."

"I love you too," she said as her eyes locked with his. Time stood still as they stood lost in each other's gaze. Their faces drew closer, and her lips met his. His lips felt amazing, so soft and loving.

With slow, gentle movements, he reached up and brushed back a strand of hair that had blown across her face. "Sarah, you mean the world to me," he said gently. "You have no idea how much I love you."

Sarah swallowed back emotions. "I've never felt this way towards anyone, Chase; I've never felt so connected. Even when we were apart, I couldn't get you out of my mind."

He smiled. "Me either." He kissed her more.

In that moment, just as the moon reflected against the water and a pelican swam over the reflection, Sarah felt something she had never felt her entire life: she felt safe and secure. She was finally home.

THE END.

ACKNOWLEDGMENTS

To my mother and brother: Your never-ending support for me and my writing projects through the years is incredible. I am so grateful for your feedback, ideas, and encouragement. Thanks, Mom, for lining the walls with paper so I could write my ideas as they came. Bryan: thank you for letting me bounce my wild ideas off you. I appreciate everything you guys have done for me–there are just too many to list here. I wouldn't have been able to do this without your support. I love you guys.

To Eric, my wonderful ~~boyfriend~~, ~~fiancé~~, husband (this book has been in progress a long time!) who endured many times of me zoning out into book-land: I appreciate the sacrifices you made so that I could write this book. Thank you for creating my website, helping me with the book cover ideas, and supporting me through this process. But most of all, thanks for showing me that selfless love exists and for providing inspiration for me to fulfill my dream of writing this book.

Patricia "Pat" Garner: When you read the first chapter of this book, you wrote two words: "Keep writing." This inspired me to keep writing and to keep pushing through the long nights and times when I struggled to describe the scenes I saw in my head. Thank you for encouraging me and for your time in editing this book. I am grateful to you for everything that you have done to make this book possible. Thank you.

To Chris Ford, Shermeen Amin, Carolyn Byrd, and Camila Pulgar: thank you guys for encouraging me to pick this project back up after years of abandonment and to see it through to completion. Thank you, Chris, for the pep talk on never underestimating myself and helping me to see that, even though there are thousands of writers, there is only one DL Hays and she has something interesting to say. Thank you, Shermeen, for your constant enthusiasm and encouragement throughout this process. Carolyn and

Camila: Thank you for always believing in me.

Thank you, Nancy and Les for your help with this book as well.

To Mayceonna, Hugh, and Jackman: thank you guys for providing comical relief during the most serious points of writing this book.

Thank you to my friends and family members who supported me through this multi-year project (there are too many to list here!). Your support did not go unnoticed and it is greatly appreciated.

ABOUT THE AUTHOR

D.L. Hays grew up in a small town in North Carolina. Becoming bored with the humdrum nature of this rarely-changing environment, she created fictional stories in order to entertain her brother and herself. Some of these stories later turned into novels.

She attended the University of North Carolina at Greensboro where she studied English Composition before switching her major to Psychology in order to "develop better fictional characters."

Graduating *summa cum laude*, DL Hays began a career in scientific research (examining human memory) and later transitioned to Industrial Organizational Psychology as a human capital consultant. Outside of business hours, D. L. Hays uses her background in psychology to help domestic violence survivors, children of inmates, senior citizens, homeless, and immigrants. These interactions inspired many of the stories that she writes.

In her spare time, D.L. Hays sails, mountain bikes, hikes, swims, skis, and trains her Australian Cattle Dog. She is often seen spending time with her husband or hanging out with family and friends.

Feel free to visit her website: www.dlhays.com to learn more about her upcoming books (including a sequel to this one) and to read her blog.

www.ingramcontent.com/pod-product-compliance
Lightning Source LLC
Chambersburg PA
CBHW030331200626
46816CB00006BA/2010